The sight of Harrison left her breathless

He completely filled the room with his broad shoulders and tall frame. And he practically pulsated with an animal magnetism that made her break out in a very feminine sweat.

His white designer shirt and olive-colored pants looked out of place next to the kitchen's dingy linoleum and gold-speckled Formica. Only the strained look on his handsome face and finger-mussed, dark gold hair kept him from looking like he'd just stepped out of his country club.

Then he turned toward her and caught her gaze. As terrified as she was by what he might say or do, she couldn't tear her gaze from his. Why did she feel so connected to him? So in tune that she swore she could feel his heartbeat throbbing through her from three feet away? Didn't her body know how dangerous he was to her? With a snap of his fingers he could take away her reason for living—her baby boy.

Not to mention what he could do to her heart…

I0645902

Dear Reader,

Welcome to Harlequin American Romance, where our goal is to give you hours of unbeatable reading pleasure.

Kick starting the month is another enthralling installment of THE CARRADIGNES: AMERICAN ROYALTY continuity series. In Michele Dunaway's *The Simply Scandalous Princess*, rumors of a tryst between Princess Lucia Carradigne and a sexy older man leads to the king issuing a royal marriage decree! Follow the series next month in Harlequin Intrigue.

Another terrific romance from Pamela Browning is in store for you with *Rancher's Double Dilemma*. When single dad Garth Colquitt took one look at his new nanny's adorable baby girl, he knew there had to be some kind of crazy mix-up, because his daughter and her daughter were twins! Was a marriage of convenience the solution? Next, don't miss *Help Wanted: Husband?* by Darlene Scarlera. When a single mother-to-be hires a handsome ranch hand, she only has business on her mind. Yet, before long, she wonders if he was just the man she needed—to heal her heart. And rounding out the month is Leah Vale's irresistible debut novel *The Rich Man's Baby*, in which a dashing tycoon discovers he has a son, but the proud mother of his child refuses to let him claim them for his own...unless love enters the equation.

This month, and every month, come home to Harlequin American Romance—and enjoy!

Best,

Melissa Jeglinski
Associate Senior Editor
Harlequin American Romance

THE RICH MAN'S BABY
Leah Vale

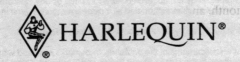

HARLEQUIN®

TORONTO • NEW YORK • LONDON
AMSTERDAM • PARIS • SYDNEY • HAMBURG
STOCKHOLM • ATHENS • TOKYO • MILAN • MADRID
PRAGUE • WARSAW • BUDAPEST • AUCKLAND

For Ross, Jake and Luke, for giving me the wings to fly.

For Maureen Child, Amy Fetzer and Tina Bilton-Smith,
for shoving me from the nest.

And for Terri Reed, Melissa Manley, Delilah Ahrent
and Kim Nadelson, for making sure I didn't splat.

ISBN 0-373-16924-8

THE RICH MAN'S BABY

ABOUT THE AUTHOR

Having never met an unhappy ending she couldn't mentally "fix," Leah Vale believes writing romance novels is the perfect job for her. A Pacific Northwest native with a B.A. in communications from the University of Washington, she lives in Portland, Oregon, with her wonderful husband, two adorable sons and a golden retriever puppy. She is an avid skier, scuba diver and "do-over" golfer. While having the chance to share her "happy endings from scratch" with the world is a dream come true, dinner generally has to come premade from the store. Leah would love to hear from her readers and can be reached at P.O. Box 91337, Portland, OR 97291, or at http://www.leahvale.com.

Books by Leah Vale

HARLEQUIN AMERICAN ROMANCE
924—THE RICH MAN'S BABY

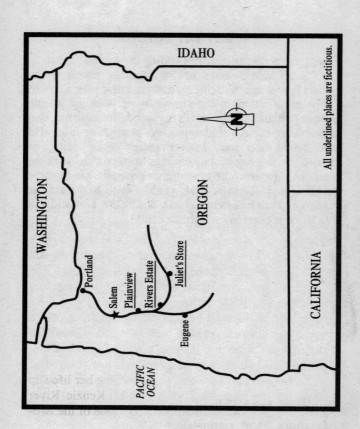

All underlined places are fictitious.

Prologue

Juliet Jones pulled in a soothing breath of warm, early-June air and leaned back in the lone wooden chair on the balcony above her family's store. After another long, boring day spent waiting behind the cash register for the rare customer to wander in, she ached clear to her bones. With a weary sigh, she slipped off her worn Keds and propped her bare feet on the peeling white railing.

She settled the cold beer bottle on the front of her frayed jeans shorts, closed her eyes and wished for the millionth time she hadn't promised Grandpa before he died that she would keep his store going. But she'd promised, so here she was watching her life slip away like the waters of Oregon's McKenzie River running steady and silent on the other side of the two-lane highway their little store hugged.

She was just twenty-one, but she felt as old as dirt.

If only Richard Gere would drive up in his Lamborghini looking just for her.

The deep growl of a motorcycle shifting down interrupted her snort at the ridiculous thought, and the sound of gravel crunching under wheels brought her eyes open. One look at the man leaning low over the green racing motorcycle as he pulled up to the store's rusting gas pump and she was a goner.

He could have a face like a butt under that black helmet and she wouldn't have cared. He looked like some mysterious warrior to her starved imagination—his black leather bomber jacket, faded blue Levi's, and trashed black cowboy boots his armor.

Juliet couldn't tell if he was looking up at her or not, so she kept staring when she would have normally looked away. She watched him settle both feet flat on the ground, turn the engine off, then reach up and flip his tinted visor up. She nearly jumped out of her skin. He was looking straight at her with beautiful, soulful eyes beneath full, dark-blond brows.

His gaze was as powerful as one of Shakespeare's love sonnets to her lonely heart.

He pulled the helmet from his head.

Juliet gaped and yanked her feet from the rail, starting a paint-chip blizzard. He was the most gorgeous man she'd ever seen. A dream come true, in fact. His straight nose and square jaw, roughened by dark-blond whiskers, held such masculine beauty she was too stunned-stupid to quit staring at him. What was a man like him doing in her world?

His gaze still on her, he hung his helmet on one of the handlebars and ran a hand through his thick, wavy, golden hair that brushed the top of his collar in the back. "Does this pump work?" he called up in a deep voice that hit her like gravel wrapped in velvet and turned her bones to liquid.

With a weak shake of her head, she croaked, "No." Clearing her throat, she needlessly added, "Though there's probably enough gas still down there to one day blow us all to kingdom come."

His smile was lopsided and unmercifully sexy. "Then you better hop on and let me take you far away from here," he offered, patting the back of his bike.

She laughed in an idiotic, high-pitched way. Man, she'd never made *that* noise before. Her face heated, and she wished she could disappear. So much for this fantasy coming true. The Adonis on the bike sure as heck wouldn't want to mess with a bubblehead on a balcony.

But instead of slapping on his helmet and roaring away, he lowered the kickstand with the heel of his boot and swung a long, thickly muscled leg over the bike and got off. "Well, if I can't top off my tank and you won't let me whisk you to safety, can I buy myself a beer inside and join you up there? I'm sure the view is something I wouldn't want to miss."

The suggestiveness of his tone and his masculine magnetic pull flustered her so much she started to ramble. "We haven't been allowed to sell beer since that incident with those darn thirteen-year-olds a couple years back. And as far as the view goes, the blackberry bushes and ash trees on the other side of the road have grown so much you can hardly see the river anymore."

He grinned up at her, and she actually felt the earth moving. But instead of making her feel wild and out of control, her heart rate slowed and everything became crystal clear. For once she knew exactly what she wanted. For once she was willing to take a risk.

She leaned forward in the chair and rested her elbows on her bare knees, with the neck of the full beer bottle caught between her fingers. Looking at him through the crooked railing, she said, "I can't sell you a beer, but you're welcome to share mine."

An intense, almost desperate look replaced his grin. "How do I get up there?"

She shook her head, sending her long, sun-streaked brown hair slipping off her shoulders. The peace of certainty made her feel powerful. "I'll come down."

"Good. Because in case you haven't noticed, that balcony has a definite lean to it. I'm not sure it's any safer than the gas pump."

This time she laughed for real. "I know. But it's *my* balcony." Thinking of her older brother's home-made racing motorcycle, she grinned and added, "Hey, if you like bikes, there's something you've got to see out back in the shed." As she rose from the chair, Juliet fought to control the surge of excitement pumping through her veins.

For the first time in her life she might actually get what she wanted.

Chapter One

Over Two Years Later...

It was her.

Surprise brought Harrison Rivers to a halt in the little store's doorway so fast the rickety screen hit his backside.

Before he could stop himself, he blurted, "You're here."

He hadn't really expected her to still be here. Especially when he'd failed to see the soles of two sexy bare feet propped on the balcony's sorry railing when he'd arrived.

Her beautiful, brown-and-gold eyes wide, she opened and closed her mouth twice before breathily answering, "I'm always here."

"I didn't think you would be."

If anyone had asked him why he was there on this sunny, September afternoon he would have claimed to have stopped for gum, but he had really made the thirty minute drive up to the little, nameless store on a backwoods Oregon highway for the first time in two years, two months, and 28 days to banish her from his thoughts. He'd hoped to find closure, even in her absence, before returning to his family estate in the nearest town of Plainview.

She ran a hand up and down her jeans-clad hip, drawing his gaze to her sexy, lean curves. "Why did you think that?"

Since he'd come back to forget her, getting turned on by her was the last thing he wanted. He forced his gaze to her face, though on his way up he couldn't keep from noticing that her breasts under her plain white T-shirt looked fuller than he remembered.

He cleared his throat. "I just assumed you'd headed off for Eugene and college. Maybe even got married." A treasure like her didn't stay buried long.

Yet here he was, staring into the same beautiful brown-and-gold eyes. They still reminded him of sunflowers lying on rich, moist earth. And he remembered too well how he'd thought at the time: *Now, maybe that's all I really want out of life—a beautiful, barefoot girl in cutoff jeans, the summer sun glinting off her honey-brown hair as she sips a beer and meditates life, the river her mantra.*

That day when she'd invited him to share her drink and her peace, he'd found himself taking more. God, how he'd needed the comfort she'd unwittingly given him. That had been so unlike him, so irresponsible, yet so right.

The wildness that had made him sample her full, luscious lips more than two years ago erupted within him like a long-dormant volcano. She was still as desirable. More so, with time adding fullness to her figure and maturity to her finely shaped face. And she was still barefoot.

Her earthy sensuality ratcheted his temperature up a few degrees.

She stepped toward him. "I didn't do any of those things. I've been here—" She stopped herself, but the word *waiting* hung between them.

Harrison met her hopeful gaze.

Damn it. He was no Prince Charming come to rescue the beautiful girl from the cinders or the glass coffin or whatever. Far from it. There was no place in his life for fairy tales.

He lowered his chin and willed her with his gaze to understand that he was doing the best thing for both of them. "I'd really hoped you had gone off to college or gotten married."

The glow in her eyes faded and the small smile curving her full lips fell. He'd made his point.

He suddenly became very aware of his Italian loafers. The reminder of how different his existence was from her barefooted freedom hit him like a bucket of ice. Before he'd said goodbye to her over two years ago, the realities of his world had forced him to acknowledge that their day together could be no more than his favorite memory.

He'd told himself it was because they were too different, having come from very opposite worlds. And he'd since vowed to never care about someone so much he lost control of his emotions.

This trip up here had been to remind him of that so he could stop thinking about her. He was determined to focus entirely on the multimillion-dollar corporation he was about to take over from his father. The company Harrison's grandfather had started and bequeathed to him as his legacy. The legacy Harrison had worked so hard to earn.

Enough eyebrows were raising on the company's board of directors as it was. His father's decision to make Harrison CEO at the ripe age of thirty-two hadn't gone over well. Even if he could control his emotions around her, Harrison wouldn't allow his judgment to be questioned by becoming involved with a woman from such a different background as his. As it was, pulling teeth was easier than getting the board to see reason and agree to his plan to purchase, shut down, then overhaul the Dover Creek Mill.

Harrison had no choice but to snuff out the shining hope in her expression.

Sometimes he really hated reality.

But he had to face the truth. With his father's retirement less than a month away, Two Rivers Industries required Harrison's undivided attention. He needed to be in total control of himself to have total control of the company. And he wasn't in control, with memories of that one time with this woman plaguing him, distracting him from what he'd been born to do—run Two Rivers Industries.

It had been a mistake to come back. The way she still pulled at him confirmed it wasn't just their differences that should have kept him away. He should leave. Nothing, after all, had changed. As he pushed open the screen door, strange regret flooded him and he hesitated. How did one say goodbye to a memory?

Before he could decide, he caught the flash of something coming at him from the side the second before it hit him in the knees. "Whoa." He looked down and saw an overalls-clad, towheaded toddler wedged between his legs. He smiled and put his big hand lightly on the little head, flattening down the riot of crazy baby hair. ''Well, hello, there.''

The face that tilted to look at him made his breath stick in his throat. The dark-green eyes warily regarding him made his heart skip a beat. The child's face seemed vaguely familiar.

The little boy stepped back, intent on making a break for the still-open door, but the sight of his red licorice rope firmly stuck to the knee of Harrison's olive-colored slacks stopped him cold and made Harrison laugh out loud.

The sound brought those solemn green eyes back up to his, and he was treated to the most cherubic smile he'd ever seen. He bent and removed the sticky candy from his pant leg, then crouched down and offered the rope to the equally sticky baby.

The little fellow snatched his candy and ran for the safety of the legs belonging to the woman Harrison had been haunted by since he'd found that moment of peace in her arms.

His heart slammed to a stop and his gaze met and held hers as she hoisted the little boy onto her hip. She hugged the child to her like a mother.

Harrison pulled in a sharp breath when he realized where he'd seen that baby's face before. Every morning he walked by a framed photo of a shockingly similar face that sat on top of his grandmother's piano.

The picture of himself as a baby.

NOT A BIT OF AIR remained in Juliet's lungs. Now she knew how a trout felt in the bottom of a boat. All that was missing was her flopping around, and if he kept staring at her like he was, that's just what she'd do.

It was him.

And here she'd thought enough time had passed that she wouldn't know him in a crowd. But the second he had walked in, she'd realized she had stored away the memory of every line on his heart-stopping, handsome face down to the tiny scar beneath his chin, every gesture he had made, and every way he had touched her.

It all came rushing back along with buckets of air. Her body clenched, then throbbed with remembered desire, and her vision swam. She squeezed Nat tight against her until he squawked and squirmed to get down.

Not wanting to let him go, but having no choice since she was about to drop him, she let the baby slide down her leg to the floor and he was off and running. Straight back to his father.

The man who had just made it clear he wanted nothing to do with her.

Oh, sweet Lord.

He squatted down again to get nose to nose with Nat and then they both looked toward her with the same eyes—the color of the river at its deepest—the same gently flared nose, the same cleft chin, the same everything. Juliet felt like she'd been punched in the stomach.

The look he gave her now nearly sent her down for the count.

He knew.

Heat rushed to her face and she could no longer meet his gaze. She glanced to the windows, looking for his motorcycle, but all she could see through the filmy glass was a sleek, black Porsche.

Her gaze flew back to his clothes. The fabric and style of his slacks and white dress shirt reeked of designer wear the way a trash bin reeked of garbage. His classy clothes perfectly set off his golden tan—the sort a guy would get out on a golf course, not digging ditches. His thick, blond hair was shorter and had been styled into submission by stylists who obviously knew what they were doing. And the gold-and-silver watch on his wrist looked exactly like the kind they gave away as a grand prize on game shows. In other words, he looked like money.

That early summer day, more than two years ago, he'd only looked like a dream on a bike.

Juliet clamped her back teeth together and straightened to her full height. He hadn't come back for her like she'd fantasized. He'd flat out said he'd wished she'd gotten married and left town. But she hadn't because of her promise to her grandfather to tend the store and because she'd never been able to forget the father of her child.

She met his gaze again, and the message she sent him said, *He's not yours.*

He glanced at Nathan, who was busily inspecting his father's legs for any other sign of licorice, then slowly looked back at her. His message read, *Like hell.*

Her heart raced and she couldn't breathe again. "Nathan, come here to Mama."

Not used to such a tone, her baby simply stared at her. They both stared at her.

She forced herself to take a deep, calming breath. What was she getting so worked up for? This man wasn't going to give a darn about her baby. Actually, she was surprised the door wasn't hitting his butt as he hauled it out of there. But in reality, he didn't look like he wanted to leave at all, now that he'd seen Nathan.

He returned his attention to Nathan with deliberate casualness and started a game of "got your nose" with him, and her heart pounded harder. What if he took a liking to her angel? He was rich, she was poor. She didn't have to be Einstein to realize how things would go if he decided he wanted her baby.

Dear Lord. Nathan was all she had.

"Hey, Natter, Big Bird's on!" her brother hollered from in the house. "Nat!" Willie continued as he came through the door that had once led to a store-room, but was now her family's living room, or more accurately, TV room. "Where are you, ya li'l booger?"

Juliet turned her back on the man she had dreamed of being with again and growled at her brother, "You were supposed to be watching him, William."

Her use of his proper name stopped him as if she'd yanked his chain, and his hazel gaze jumped to her. As usual, her big, lazy, older brother's short brown hair stuck flat to his head on one side and stood straight up on the other, and he had his red-and-black flannel shirt misbuttoned.

"What'd he do?" Willie quickly scanned the store till he spotted the toddler. "You botherin' the customers again, booger?"

"Don't call him that," she ground out. "I've told you a thousand times."

Nat's father said, "He's not bothering anyone." He rumpled Nat's too-long hair.

Ohh, how she remembered his deep, rumbly voice that had turned her to mush in a heartbeat. And the sweet words of flattery and destiny he'd whispered in her ear. And how she had allowed herself, just that once, to believe. To believe in knights in shining armor and princesses who lived happily ever after.

"But I bet you like to bother ants, don'tcha?" he asked her baby and stood. "Just like your daddy."

"Who knows?" Willie said as he went toward them. "Natter's daddy was just some guy on a sweet bike who stopped only long enough to disappear in the back shed with my little sister."

"William!"

"It's not like it's any big secret." Willie scooped up his nephew and tossed the little boy on his broad shoulder. She thought Nat's daddy was about to protest until he appeared to realize that the squeals the child made were ones of pleasure.

"So you thought that bike was sweet, eh?" he asked Willie.

"Yeah, I did."

"So did I," he said with a wistful smile that sent a jolt of longing through Juliet.

She closed her eyes and fisted her hands at her sides. Maybe if she concentrated real hard this would all go away.

Willie was halfway to the back of the store before what the guy had said registered. "Say what?"

Nat's father let out a soft breath. "Boy, that thing could move. But what do you expect from a Beemer? I could have done without the fluorescent green, though." He said it all so offhandedly, like her brother already knew that he was the guy on the bike.

Juliet's eyes snapped open. Clearly he wanted him

to know. No, no, no. He'd already made his feelings toward her clear. He would only want Nathan.

"You knew that bike?" Willie asked as he started back toward the handsome man by the door.

"Of course." With his hands buried casually in his pockets, he looked for all the world as if they were chatting about the weather.

Her brother frowned fiercely. "How?"

Willie was so dumb. He had been the only other person around that day, though he had been too interested in the green-and-white BMW racing motorcycle to notice his little sister falling head-over-heels for the guy who had climbed off the thing. But she'd just turned twenty-one at the time, so she doubted his notice would have mattered much anyhow.

Her one and only mistake's expression grew serious. "Because it was mine."

"What?" Willie exclaimed.

Extending a hand toward her brother, he said, "The name's Harrison Rivers."

Harrison. His name was Harrison *Rivers,* of all things. She would have remembered a name like that. So he really hadn't told her. Her fantasies were unraveling more and more by the second.

His gaze locked on hers as he said to her brother, "I was the guy in the back shed with your sister."

"No!" Harrison's brown-eyed girl practically shouted the denial. She swiftly moved forward and reached for his child.

My God. He had a child. His chest felt ready to explode with emotions he couldn't name or begin to control.

He watched her perch the baby on her slim hip and

tuck his little head under her chin. "This isn't the guy." She stared him in the eye, daring him to argue.

"Are you sure?" her brother asked, eyeing Harrison from head to foot.

"Of course I'm sure. Don't you think I'd know?" she said sharply.

"You heard what I said." Harrison stated quietly what his heart wanted to shout, "That baby is mine." Then his throat closed up. They'd made a baby that day. All this time he'd thought they'd only made a little magic, a little bit of heaven that wasn't meant to last.

His baby's mother gulped like she was swallowing something distasteful. "No. No he is *not*," she clearly lied, her face growing paler by the second.

Harrison captured her gaze again. Why was she denying this? He would have thought a woman in her circumstances would be pointing a finger at him and screeching, *This is the guy who knocked me up!*

"Then how did he know about the bike?" her brother asked, still unconvinced.

Her breath started coming so hard Harrison could hear it from where he stood. "Ah, lucky guess?" she fumbled, refusing to meet his eyes.

Harrison's heart went out to her for what she must have gone through, pregnant and alone, but he wasn't going to let her deny him. That child was part of him.

"Why would he be claiming to be the guy if he's not *the guy?*" her brother argued. Maybe he wasn't as mentally challenged as he looked.

"Why?" she parroted. She started shifting her weight from one bare foot to the other.

Man, she still had sexy feet. His body responded instantly with all sorts of throbbing and hardening.

Just as it had over two years ago. Only, now he couldn't blame his reaction to her on his grief and the way it had made him so out of control. So why did she still push all his hot buttons just standing there with bare feet?

He gave himself a shake and promised *not* to find out. He had never reacted to any woman the way he did to her, and instant fatherhood was complication enough.

"Why?" she repeated. "How the heck should I know? Maybe he's some kind of pervert who wants to get his hands on Nat." Her desperation became glaringly obvious in the way she struggled for an argument.

Again he found himself wondering why she wanted to negate his responsibility. Could she be so selfless as to want to spare him? But why would she think he wanted to be spared?

He asserted, "I am not a pervert. I'm a man who takes responsibility for his mistakes."

Her eyes flared, and he instantly regretted his choice of words.

"My child is not a mistake," she hissed.

He raised his hands in supplication. "I'm sorry. You know what I meant."

"You're right, I do. Just like I know what you meant when you said earlier that you'd hoped I'd gotten married and left town. So why don't you head on back down the highway like you'd planned."

"I can't. Not now."

"Wow." Her brother laughed in disbelief.

"No, no, no," she whispered, and slowly backed away.

Harrison pointed at the child. "Just look at him.

He looks exactly like me. There are pictures of me as a baby on my grandmother's piano. That's what I looked like at…what? About eighteen months?'' he asked the brother and received a nod in answer. ''He looks just like me because I'm his father. I came through here the beginning of June over two years ago and saw the most beaut— I saw you, sitting up on that balcony, and, well, I lost my head.''

''And got something else,'' her brother mumbled crudely.

Harrison glared into William's hazel eyes, nowhere near the deep color of his sister's, and thought if he had been her brother, he would have flattened the man who'd left his sister pregnant by now. But this idiot looked downright amused.

She didn't. She looked…scared? What did she have to be afraid of? The only thing he was sure of at that moment was that he intended to accept his responsibilities, as he'd been raised to do, for this child. His child.

Holy smoke.

The spark back in her mesmerizing brown-and-gold eyes, she said challengingly, ''What makes you think you weren't just one of a ton of guys who've… who've ridden through here?''

''Nobody's gonna buy that, Julie,'' her brother said, butting in. He turned to Harrison. ''She's not like that. As far as anyone knows that's the only time she's even let a guy get close,'' he said, defending her with an odd sort of pride.

Harrison blanched, vividly remembering his shock when he'd discovered she had been a virgin—after she no longer was one. She had been adamant that it had been her choice, that she had wanted him to be the one. A distinction that even now stirred something vaguely possessive within him. He'd never felt possessive about any woman before, which was why he'd known even then that he shouldn't see her again. But now things were different. He had a son.

William gave his sister a fond look. "Fellas 'round here don't call Julie the ice princess for nothing."

She gave him a virulent glare in return and growled, "You are such dead meat, Willie. I already said, *He's not the guy.*"

Harrison willed her to look at him again, but she buried her face in the sleepy toddler's soft hair. "Your name's not Julie," he half whispered, racking his brain for the name that floated just beyond his reach. It was more lyrical than Julie.

His inability to remember her name bothered him. But names hadn't been important then. They had stepped to a different plane where such things didn't matter. The only thing that had mattered was the connection he had felt to her the second their gazes had met. The connection that tugged at him still.

Finally she looked up into his eyes, and it hit him. "Juliet. Your name is Juliet."

Her eyes welled and a single tear spilled down her cheek. His throat closed up again. She turned and ran with the child through the door to the back. Apparently, for her the connection had broken. For some inexplicable reason his pride felt pricked.

"That's right," her brother exclaimed. As he turned to follow his sister he added, "But everyone around here calls her Julie."

Harrison shook his head. He would never call her that. Despite the fact there could never be anything other than parenthood between them again.

Chapter Two

"You *what?*" Harrison's father, George Rivers, roared and jumped to his feet, nearly toppling his chair.

Harrison raised his eyes to the study's high, coffered ceiling and willed himself to stay calm. "I said, I just discovered I'm the father of an adorable, eighteen-month-old boy," he repeated, annoyed by the slight tremor of emotion in his voice. He would have to get a handle on that and soon. He had to keep his perspective to make rational decisions.

Unfortunately, he suspected that little boy had already undermined his determination to keep his emotions under control. Nathan was one more person Harrison had to fear losing—one more person with the power to change him like his father had been changed.

His father put his fists on the desk and leaned forward. "The hell you say. Who is she? You haven't taken the time to see anyone from around here. Is she one of your classmates from Harvard?"

"Her name is Juliet Jones. And no, she didn't attend Harvard."

"Juliet? I don't remember meeting any Juliet." His

father straightened and ran a weary hand over his balding head, massaging it as he went. "I don't recall hearing you so much as mention a Juliet."

"That's because you didn't meet her and I am certain I never mentioned her." Harrison walked to the floor-to-ceiling windows lining one wall of the study.

He braced his hands against the frame and gazed out at the expanse of freshly cut lawn and a wall of manicured shrubs. That time with Juliet had been his most private—not to mention distracting—memory. Having to make it known rankled, but he would do what was right.

"How long were you involved with this girl?"

Harrison's jaw tightened as he faced his father. "One day." One incredible, *fateful* day.

His father's brows rose to where his hair had once been and he flushed vividly. "Are you saying this was a one-night stand? My God, Harrison. You've always pushed the envelope, but you've never done anything stupid before."

"George, stop badgering the boy and let him tell us about the baby," Harrison's paternal grandmother finally spoke up from her chair in front of the fireplace.

George raised his hands in submission and sat back down behind his desk. "All right, all right." Gesturing to Harrison, he said with a sarcastic note, "Please. Continue. I'm dying to hear about any and all of your illegitimate offspring."

"Damn it, Dad—"

"Gentlemen, please." Dorothy Rivers rose and came toward them. Elegantly diminutive, she looked up at Harrison with warm green eyes. "Darling, do get back to telling us about the baby and this Juliet."

Harrison blew out a breath. "Yes, of course, Grandmother." He took her small hand in his and used the excuse of leading her to one of the chairs in front of the great mahogany desk to reclaim his temper.

His father made a rude noise. "Exactly how much do you know about this woman?"

Harrison helped his grandmother get seated then faced his father. "Not much. Her family lives above and in the rooms behind a store they operate up on the McKenzie River."

His father crimsoned. "Are you telling us you knocked up a storekeeper's daughter?"

"George, don't be crude."

Harrison frowned. "As far as I could tell today, she's the one who does the keeping." He wished he had found out more, but Juliet had refused to speak further with him. Her brother, suddenly acquiring a proper brotherly attitude, would only answer the most basic questions about his sister and nephew.

"So why did she wait so long to contact you?" his father asked. "You did say the child was eighteen months old, didn't you?"

"Yes, he is. And she didn't contact me. I found out about him when I went back to the store—"

His father sat forward. "You went back? Why? You said it was a one-night stand."

"Yes, I went back, and why is none of your business. If I hadn't I never would have known about Nathan."

His grandmother sat forward, too. "His name is Nathan?"

Harrison smiled into her eyes, only slightly faded

by age, and nodded. "Nathan Maxwell Jones. Apparently, she named him after her grandfather."

"Just like you were. Is he a towhead like you were, too?" Her eyes positively sparkled now.

Harrison's smile widened. "As blond as can be." He felt an intense warmth he wasn't inclined to squelch spread through his chest when he pictured the little boy. *His* little boy.

George gave him that narrow-eyed look he'd been using at the office. "Is this Juliet aware of how much you're worth?"

Harrison glared right back. "Seeing as I left my business card with her brother, I don't think it'd be too hard to figure out."

His father tented his fingers in front of him, his high forehead creased in displeasure.

Harrison raised his hands in exasperation. "What difference does it make? I'm going to do the right thing in regards to my child."

His father slowly rose to his feet. "And just what do you consider 'the right thing' to be?"

Harrison shrugged at the obviousness of the answer. "To provide for my son and become a part of his life, as any father should."

His grandmother's eyes went wide. "You mean through marriage?"

Harrison pulled back his chin, not having thought of his involvement in those terms at all. To say Juliet wasn't exactly corporate wife material would be putting it mildly. Their differences were too great for that sort of relationship. Besides, he didn't want any kind of relationship. No matter how much he was attracted to her, he could never let himself have her again.

His father scoffed. "Of course he doesn't mean

through marriage.'' He waved the idea off then fixed Harrison with a hard look. ''What kind of proof did she give that you are indeed the father? No way will I acknowledge some random child as a member of the Rivers family without proof.''

Not about to give his father ammunition by telling him about Juliet's claim that someone else fathered Nathan, he said, ''She doesn't need any proof. All you have to do is look at Nat to know he's mine. *I* know he's mine.'' That baby was tangible proof of the intangible connection he'd felt with Juliet. A connection the likes of which he had never felt before or since.

''And all she has to do is look at you to know she's hit the jackpot.''

''Juliet thinks no such thing. She made it quite clear she doesn't want anything from me.'' Just as he'd made it clear he wanted nothing more from her before he'd met Nathan. An image of her in her snug T-shirt, jeans and bare feet came to mind, and his body instantly responded. Too bad it was a lie. Good thing lust could be ignored.

''Well, if she's not making any claim, you certainly aren't obligated—''

Harrison fisted his hands at his sides as a cold, suffocating anger surged through him. ''It doesn't matter if she's making a claim or not. That child is *of* me. And obligated or not, I plan to be a part of his life and to make his life better for it. End of discussion.''

He turned to leave, but his grandmother's soft touch on his hand stopped him. She placed an emerald silk-clad elbow on the arm of the chair and leaned toward him, an intense expression in her mossy eyes. "Do you intend to make a claim on the child?"

Harrison raised his brows. "You mean sue for custody?"

Only one of her brows went up in response.

His father put his head in his hands and groaned, "Good God."

Harrison shook his head. "No. That would be wrong."

From behind his hands George said, "And you're the expert on that, aren't you? Getting a girl you don't even know pregnant and all."

Harrison gave his father a narrow-eyed look of his own. "At least I'm prepared to deal with it," he shot back before he turned and left the room. Taking Nathan away from his mother would definitely be wrong. The notion hadn't even occurred to him.

Then the image of the store came to mind. The place was falling apart. No one would blame him for wanting to take his baby out of those conditions. He stopped in the foyer and looked around. Nowhere could be more perfect for raising a child than the opulent but extremely livable Rivers estate. He had loved growing up here.

Knowing the importance of family, his grandfather had wanted his son and grandchildren close to him, so he'd had this huge house built, with separate wings providing each part of the family with their own space. And Harrison needed every inch of that space when his father was in one of the *moods* he had begun to suffer in the past two years. If not for his grandmother and his younger sister, Ashley, Harrison would have bought a condo in town close to work. Were he to ever move, though, he would miss the place, and Harrison knew Nathan would love living here.

But he refused to take a child away from his mother. He remembered the way Juliet hugged Nat's little body close to hers, tucking his head beneath her chin. Clearly she loved his son. She didn't deserve to lose Nathan simply because her family lived in near poverty. Besides, he could never willfully annihilate the *rightness* of their one time together by portraying her as unsuitable.

The answer sprang to mind and sent his pulse racing. No one said he had to take Nathan away from Juliet for him to be raised here. Whether she wanted anything from Harrison or not, he decided to convince Juliet that some very drastic changes needed to be made in her life.

Willing his pulse back to normal, Harrison strode toward the front door and left the house, feeling once more in control.

There might be a tiny pinch of Prince Charming lurking somewhere in his calculating corporate soul after all.

JULIET STUCK HER FINGERS in her ears, squeezed her eyes shut so tight she saw little white lights and hummed the National Anthem, but it didn't work. It never did. No matter how hard she tried, her family wouldn't go away. She should have learned by now that wishing them away didn't work, but it never hurt to try. With a soul-weary sigh she dropped her hands into her lap and opened her eyes.

She looked from her mother, with a bad perm sticking out every which way from her head, to her brother, whose filthy red baseball hat was turned backward, as always.

As they sat around the kitchen table, Mom and Willie were talking over each other. They both had an opinion about what she should do now that the father of her child had suddenly reappeared. And neither one of them had asked her opinion.

Well, she had one.

"Will you please listen to me for a minute?" she pleaded, but failed to draw their attention. "Excuse me!" she said loud enough to cut through the noise about a father's responsibilities and child-support settlements.

They looked at her for the first time since the discussion began. "Weren't you listening when I told you this…" She had to take a deep, steadying breath before she could say the name of the man she had once foolishly thought to be her soul mate. "…Harrison Rivers is not Nathan's father?"

"Oh, get off it, Julie," Willie said. "Any idiot can see the kid's his."

Frustration getting the better of her, she retorted, "And that qualifies *you,* doesn't it?"

"Stop it, you two," her mother snapped.

"He knew about the bike, didn't he?" Willie gave a curt nod of his head. "That's proof enough for me."

Her mom shifted toward her, the plastic seat cover beneath her squeaking. "Men don't go around claiming to be babies' fathers without cause, Julie." She reached across the yellowed, gold-speckled Formica table and put a hand on Juliet's forearm. "Why do you keep denying he's the father? From what your brother says, he seems decent enough."

"And stinkin' rich," Willie added. "He's got serious bucks. I talked to that friend of mine, Dave, who used to work on the loading dock at Two Rivers Industries, which was the name of the company on the business card he left, and Dave said that if Julie's guy is—''

"He's not my guy," Juliet grumbled. How could she lay claim to a man like that? And since no fairy godmother was going to bibbidi-bop into her life and change her into someone he would want, she had no choice but to deny he was the one. She couldn't lose Nathan.

"He sure was your guy for…what, fifteen minutes?" Willie laughed then winked crudely at her.

She smacked him on the arm and made him squawk.

"Stop it, you two."

"Anyway," Willie continued, "if this guy is the same Harrison Rivers who's taking over the company so his dad can retire, he's worth *millions*." Willie said it like he was imparting the secret of life, then got up and went to the fridge.

The implications of his words hit Juliet full on. Her stomach rolled, and she had to swallow fast to keep from being sick all over the kitchen table.

Then she started to shake. The tremors were small at first, deep in her chest. But as Willie's words echoed in her head and both pairs of eyes in the cramped kitchen fastened on her, the reverberations spread throughout her like oil in a mud puddle.

Millions. Harrison Rivers had millions.

Her mother's normally dour face lit up with excitement as a thought occurred to her. "Maybe you could pick up with him where you left off!"

Juliet could barely speak. "He's already said he doesn't want me."

Tsking, her mother shook her head, then heaved a dramatic sigh. "You realize, don't you, that takes this thing to a whole new level?"

"Oh, yeah," Willie concurred as he brought a beer back to the table.

Of course it took things to a whole new level. The level with high-priced lawyers and bought-off caseworkers. The level where someone like her could never stand a chance against someone like him. The level where all her tears and pleas would carry about as much weight as a foam anchor.

Why couldn't he have been some average guy who might have decided he wanted her for more than one afternoon of fun? A regular Joe-shmoe she could have had a future with.

Before the tremors building inside of her reached a crescendo and she shattered right there in front of them, Juliet shoved back her metal-legged chair, its legs screeching along the floor, and bolted to her feet. "It doesn't take this *thing* anywhere," she choked out. "Because there's nothing there in the first place. Nat's mine. Nobody else's. Mine!" She slammed her open hand down on the tabletop and glowered at her mom and Willie, huddled around the table like a couple of witches around their pot.

"If you're going to act like *that* you surely won't have a say in what we decide to do," her mother reprimanded.

Willie offered, "I think we should be talking maternity suit."

Juliet ground her teeth. "That's what you wear when you're pregnant and have to go to work."

He nodded. "Right, right. What we should be discussing here is a maternity *settlement.*"

Juliet threw her hands in the air. "Paternity. *Paternity settlement.* Don't be such an idiot."

"You're the idiot," he jeered.

"Stop it, you two."

Willie grumbled, "At least you were smart enough to get knocked up by a millionaire."

Juliet went to the sink and leaned her weight on her hands on the rim. The distorted view of the sunset silhouetting the back shed out the small, cracked window above the sink began to swim as tears filled her eyes once again. She hadn't been smart at all, letting herself believe in a dream on a bike.

"I'm not sure a paternity settlement is the way to go, Julie," her mom answered as if Juliet had thrown those words out as an option she would consider. "I think, personally, that child support payments are—"

"No, no," Willie interrupted. "I think the guy should hand over a huge chunk of change up front now, while he's still all doe-eyed over finding his kid."

The image of Harrison crouched before her son with a sticky length of red licorice in his hand and an enraptured smile on his handsome face made Juliet groan softly. Then that image shifted and became Harrison hovering above her, his river-green eyes murky with passion.

She remembered how she'd buried her hands in his lush, golden hair and pulled him down for a kiss. He'd kissed her soft and slow, like he'd known kissing wasn't something she'd done a lot of, like he'd been coaxing a smoldering ember to flame. And, oh, how she'd flamed.

His mouth had felt like chocolate just starting to melt. His hard, flat stomach had been so hot upon hers she'd thought he'd cook her to the marrow. They had been so good together, so right. Like they would never part.

But they had, and now that she knew who and what he really was, they were so, so far apart. There was no way they would ever be together again like she'd dreamed. He was rich. And he'd already made it plain he didn't want her. Juliet squeezed her eyes shut and forced the memories away before turning to face her family.

Her mom shook her head, making her fuzzy curls quiver. "No, I think *monthly* child support payments would be the most profitable—"

The tension that had brought Juliet's shoulders up around her ears snapped her like a dried birch twig.

"Profitable!" She stared slack-jawed at her family. "I can't believe you actually said it! Is that all Nat is to you now? Something you can make an easy buck off? Can't you see that Harrison isn't going to hand you a wad of money and let me keep Nathan?"

She pointed a trembling finger at her brother. "Willie, you saw how he looked at Nat. He's going to want him." Her lip trembling uncontrollably, she looked between the two of them. "Don't you care that he's my baby? My world? Don't you care about either one of us?"

"Mom cares enough to give you a roof over your heads and food in your bellies so you don't have to go to work or school or anything," Willie shot back.

"So *I* don't have to work? Who do you think tends that store out there? When was the last time you stood behind the counter?"

"Hey, I'm scheduled to start on the green chain at Dover Creek," Willie protested.

Juliet ignored him. "And as far as going to school, you know I can't afford to go anywhere yet."

"How do you know, when you've never even applied to any schools or tried to get financial aid?" He found an old wound of hers and poked it.

Juliet clamped her teeth together and fought the tears blinding her and the raging swell of helplessness that threatened to strangle her.

"You don't know a thing about me," she choked out, then left the kitchen.

The frustration exploded within her, and she started running—through the living room, through the empty store, and out into the dusk-shadowed gravel parking lot. She mentally winced when the busted screen door hit the wall after she blasted through the door. She prayed the bang didn't wake her baby. But she didn't stop running. She knew if Nat cried out her mother or Willie would go to him. At least she could count on them for that.

With barely a glance in either direction at the lights of oncoming traffic, Juliet darted across the two-lane highway and plunged down the embankment. She followed the well-worn trail until it ended at the stone-strewn edge of the McKenzie River.

Taking her usual seat on a smooth boulder, she tried to focus on the dark water slipping by, to let the steadiness of the river seep into her soul and smooth the rough edges of her pain like it had smoothed the rocks around her, but her tears made it impossible. Juliet buried her face in her hands and let loose the body-racking sobs she'd been doing such a lousy job of containing.

She was being pitiful and feeling sorry for herself, but she didn't care. At this precise moment she didn't have the strength to care. She'd think of a way to keep her baby out of everyone's clutches later. Right now she just wanted to cry and curse the day she'd fallen for Harrison Rivers and taken the one and only chance of her miserable life.

Chapter Three

A blur of sun-blond hair and bare limbs dashed through Harrison's headlights. He shoved his foot down hard on the brake pedal and swore.

Thank heavens he'd already been slowing to turn off into the gravel parking lot of the little store. If he'd been going full speed, he wasn't sure he could have stopped in time. Twilight was a dangerous time to drive as it was, without crazed females bolting out in front of him.

He didn't have to look twice to know the woman who'd nearly become his hood ornament had been Juliet, but he did look to see where she entered the underbrush and disappeared over the edge of the road.

Finishing his turn into the parking lot, Harrison brought his Porsche to a stop alongside the rusted gas pump. After leaving his father and grandmother at home, he had jumped in his car and headed back up the river. He'd told himself he was coming to see his child, his boy—but after seeing Juliet blaze across the street without so much as a look-see, he acknowledged he'd come to see her. He needed to make sure she didn't hold some power over him beyond the comfort she'd unwittingly given him during his time of grief two years ago.

Getting out of his car, Harrison spared a glance at the storefront. While the white-and-red plastic sign read Open, the interior of the building stood dark except for a glow coming from the rear. Somebody better be in there, because his little boy certainly hadn't been in his momma's arms when she'd darted in front of Harrison's car.

But as he started across the parking lot toward the road, the image of Juliet tucking their baby's head under her chin flitted through his mind again. Somehow he doubted she'd leave Nathan unattended. Obviously she loved the child.

His child.

The knot that had formed in his stomach earlier today tightened. He hoped talking to Juliet about what had happened would loosen it a bit. Though her reaction to his declaration of paternity made him certain this talk wouldn't be congenial, he had to make her see he wouldn't settle for less than what was best for their son. And he firmly believed disappearing back down the highway for good wasn't in Nathan's best interest.

Taking considerably more care crossing the two-lane highway than Juliet had, Harrison jogged across the street, then started down what seemed to be a trail through the blackberry bushes and other underbrush growing on the embankment. His leather-soled loafers proved slick on the gravel-strewn dirt path, and the waning light made it difficult to pick his way down the trail, so he was forced to catch himself with his hand several times to keep from sliding down the incline on his rear.

The soft murmur of the river confirmed his suspicion of the trail's destination, right before he emerged from the bank's growth onto the rocks at the river's edge. The paleness of the stones reflected what light still hovered in the air, so Harrison had no trouble spotting Juliet. Her slender back to him, she sat huddled atop a thigh-high boulder, her arms folded on her drawn-up knees and her head resting on her forearms.

What he had initially thought was another sound of the river turned out to be Juliet crying. Her soft, soul-wrenching sobs touched him so deeply he clenched his jaw against the sensation. She was crying because of him. He knew it.

Seized with the urge to comfort her, just as he had been compelled to be a part of her two years ago so she could comfort him, Harrison made his way toward her. One of his loafers slipped off a poorly chosen rock and his foot plunged into a small, stagnant pool of orphaned river. The splash sounded like a shotgun blast.

Juliet's head jerked up and she swiveled on the rock toward him. She stared at him, her posture like a mouse caught in a hawk's sights. A full minute passed, and he was about to identify himself when she finally spoke.

"You." That one word held a wealth of recrimination and mistrust. "What do you want?"

Feeling like an invader of sanctuary, Harrison raised a hand, palm up, toward her. "We need to talk."

With stiff, jerky movements, she turned to face the river again and pulled her knees up tighter to her chest. "We have absolutely nothing to talk about."

Harrison drew in a fortifying breath of river-moistened air and started toward her once again, only to realize he still had one foot ankle-deep in water. Releasing the breath with a sigh, he extracted his sodden foot from the puddle and gave it a shake. Nothing about this was going to be easy. Absolutely nothing. But he had to make her listen. Not only for Nathan's sake, but for their sake, too. They had to put to rest what had happened between them so they could move forward as rational adults.

Not caring anymore where he stepped, Harrison moved to her side. This close, he could easily make out the features of her profile. As before, he was struck by her loveliness. Little wonder he'd never completely forgotten her. Seeing her, free from the earlier distractions, Harrison confirmed again that he'd had very good reasons for never contacting her. She was more than a threat to his vow to never care about a woman enough that he lost control of his emotions; she was an all-out assault.

Not even the hardness of her expression diminished her effect on him. Once again he found himself wanting to get lost in her, to forget about the burdens he carried, the frustrations he bore. He wanted to meld with her and not have to manage or dictate or supervise, but just be.

Damn it.

Thank God he wasn't the same irresponsible man he'd been over two years ago. He couldn't allow himself to give in to the out-of-control desire he apparently still harbored. He was stronger now. He *could* risk having her in his life. As the mother of his child. Nothing more.

"Juliet," he whispered. Her knees dropped away

from her chest an inch or two, as if the sound of her name on his lips weakened her defenses. "Juliet, please. It's just you and me here. You don't have to pretend. We need to talk about our son."

She finally looked at him, but in the failing light he couldn't identify the emotion in her tear-swollen eyes. "He's *my* son. Not ours. Not anybody's but mine."

He heard what he hadn't been able to see. The tortured strain of her voice told him what she was feeling, why she'd been crying. He wasn't surprised when she pulled her knees up tight against her again. She was feeling besieged.

"Look, Juliet, I know how you feel. I know you're afraid. Of what, I'm not exactly sure, but—"

"Oh, so you know how I feel? How is that? Considering you don't even *know* me."

His empathy beginning to give way to frustration, he leaned in close. "You and I both know how well I know you."

She jerked away from him like she'd been slapped. Harrison pulled back and let out a noisy breath. He was doing this all wrong. She would never let him help her if she stayed mad at him. He needed to make up for the damage he'd done before he found out about Nathan.

"I'm sorry, Juliet. Today has been a little trying for me, too. It's not every day a man walks into a store to buy gum and walks out a father. So forgive me if I'm not as patient or as understanding as I should be."

She turned to look at him again. "Is that the only reason you stopped? For gum?"

Harrison squinted hard at her, trying to cut through

the gloom to see what emotion swam in her dark eyes. He wanted to be sure that he had been right earlier, that she had been waiting for him to come back for her. The possibility revived the wildness he'd felt then. He did his damnedest to clamp a lid on it.

Planting his hands on his hips, he shifted his weight to his squishy, wet shoe. "Well, since I'm trying to get you to be honest, I suppose I have to tell you the truth, too." He shifted his weight back and softened the truth considerably. "No. I didn't stop to get gum. I came up here because a stupid, silly part of me was hoping to see again the beautiful, barefoot woman I'd never been able to forget."

He could just make out the narrowing of her eyes. "A stupid, silly part of you?"

So she suffered from a touch of vanity. Good. He was powerless against her stubbornness and strength of will, but vanity he could work with. Despite the fact he would be testing his control to the max, he'd have her agreeing to let him be a part of Nathan's life yet.

He leaned toward her, ignoring how her fresh, clean smell filled his head and opened the door to all sorts of physical needs. "The stupid, silly part of me who still scans the sky for eight tiny reindeer on Christmas Eve and makes a wish when I blow out my birthday candles."

Her lips parted slightly, then she tightened them and frowned. "But what about when you said you wished I had left for college and gotten married?"

"I panicked," he lied. He couldn't very well tell her he'd meant to squash the hope shining in her eyes. "You were so beautiful standing there, more beautiful than I'd remembered, and I felt like a bastard for not coming back.''

Her hold on her legs went slack and her knees dropped away from her chest again. This time nearly a foot.

He let the silence build for a while before he broke it. ''Why didn't you let me know I'd made you pregnant, Juliet? Why didn't you tell me I had a child?''

''How could I? I didn't know who you were,'' she whispered, then pulled her knees back up.

Rife with regret, he ran a hand through his hair. ''I'm sorry. I am so sorry.'' He had to make her understand that he hadn't used her, that what had happened between them hadn't been about sex. It had been about trying to focus on life instead of death, about being free of the sorrows and pressures of his existence for a moment or two.

He reached out and laid a hand on her shoulder, the material of her white T-shirt doing a poor job of keeping at bay the memory of the texture of her skin. ''I've thought about you, and our time together, a lot. It's not that I didn't want to come back…but…'' He fumbled for an explanation that wasn't as insulting as the bald truth. ''But my responsibilities made it impossible for me to come see you again.''

''Because I'm from—'' she made quotation marks in the air with her fingers ''—the wrong side of the tracks.'' Her words virtually dripped with disgust. ''I'm sort of curious. Why did you come anywhere near me in the first place?''

''It mostly had to do with my mother.'' He surprised himself with his truthful answer. He'd never talked about how his mother's death had affected him with anyone. His family knew, but they never spoke of that time. There was something about Juliet that made him step beyond the boundaries he set for himself. Something he'd avoid if he were smart.

She gave him a sarcastically doleful look. "Your mother."

Compelled to defend himself after making such a ridiculous-sounding statement, he explained, "About the time I returned home from school to start at Two Rivers, my mom was diagnosed with breast cancer. She had the most radical surgery available and came through the chemo okay, so we figured she'd be fine."

He ran a hand over his eyes and fought to push down the swell of pain. The pain was precisely why he never spoke of those terrible days. "After a couple of years, the cancer came back, though, and it spread everywhere…"

An image came to mind of his mom, pale and shaking with pain. "She used to refuse the morphine so she would be lucid enough to talk to me about how work was going when I returned home in the evening. I did my damnedest to always have good news for her.

"She was so angry with me when I refused to go to the office near the end. She wanted me to be an even bigger success running the family business than my father, but there was no way I wasn't going to be with her, to help her fight for her life."

He shook his head sadly at his inability to help her. The cancer proved stronger than his bright, vibrant mother, and she'd slipped away. "Everyone except my dad was there with her when she died. He couldn't handle seeing it happen. I couldn't handle it afterward, so I took off on my motorcycle for a week and ended up here.''

He paused, struggling to put the pain back in the dark pit where it belonged. ''It's never good to love someone so much that you lose control like that.''

He felt the warmth of her fingers, then her palm as she slipped her hand over his forearm, her touch more comforting than anything he'd ever felt. He slowly swayed toward her, wanting to wrap himself around her and absorb her like a balm for his hurt. But she broke the contact and forced him back to the difficult reality of the situation.

He shoved his hands in his pockets and cleared his throat. ''The reason I didn't come back was that I had to devote all my time and energy to running my family's paper producing company. Now that I know about Nathan, I promise, from here on out I'll do whatever I can to make everything right. I intend to be a father to Nathan. I will live up to my responsibilities and provide for him in every way. I—''

''Whoa, whoa. Hold on.'' She slid her feet off the boulder and stood. ''What do you mean, be a father to Nat? Live up to your responsibilities? Provide for him?'' Her voice gained in volume. ''If you think you can just show up here with your sad stories,'' her voice cracked, but she continued, ''after deciding my baby looks like you, and take him away, you've got another thing com—''

''Now *you* whoa. I never said anything about taking Nathan away from you.''

''Maybe not now, but later…''

''No.'' He said the words with the echo of this afternoon's conversation with his father and grandmother still in his head.

"That's right. Because you're not Nathan's father!" she shouted and turned toward the trail.

He caught hold of her arm, instinctively pulling her tight against him. He couldn't seem to touch her without wanting to touch all of her. She trembled against him, and he instantly lightened his grip to a caress. "Please, not that again. Can't you—"

"Nat and I were doing fine until you showed up." She stepped away and yanked her arm from his hand. "We don't need a thing from you."

"He needs a father."

"Well, you're not him," she stated, and headed for the path to the road.

He watched until she disappeared in the underbrush and then he buried both hands in his hair. That hadn't gone the way it should have. Not one damn bit.

He should have focused more on what he could do for Nathan, on how easily he could improve their child's life by moving them to the estate. Surely she'd want what was best for Nathan. He knew he sure as hell did, and he'd only had Nathan in his life for a day.

Unfortunately, after having Juliet back in his life for a day, he feared what was best for Nathan would not be best for Nathan's parents.

"WE GOTTA LEAVE. We gotta leave," Juliet chanted to herself in a panting whisper as she mounted the stairs to her room. Her heart slammed around in her chest, and her breath did a rotten job clearing her throat.

Forcing her mind to concentrate on what she needed to do wasn't easy with Harrison's words reverberating in her ears. *He needs a father,* he'd said.

A father who didn't want the mother. He would decide she wasn't good enough, then take her baby away.

She wouldn't let him. She would pack their things, bundle Nat up in his quilt, and go. Problem solved, she thought as she quietly opened the door and slipped into the room crowded by Nathan's crib, her narrow bed and a single dresser.

But he only said he'd wished you'd left and gone to college because he felt bad about not coming back. You might still have a chance with him.

She shook her head at such nonsense and forced the tiny voice that had kept her hopes alive back into the bruised corner of her heart where it belonged.

Quietly moving to the crib, she checked on Nat. Seeing her baby—curled in a little ball around the quilt she'd made for him, his breath coming in tiny, even huffs—eased the tightness in her throat and allowed her to breathe again. But while the tightness eased at the sight of Nat's sweet back, in its place was something as debilitating—the pain of a mother's love. She loved her child with an intensity that invaded every pore and threatened to twist her guts till they were of no use to her anymore. She couldn't lose him.

Keeping an eye on her sleeping toddler, Juliet tiptoed to the side of her bed and got down on her hands and knees. After groping about beneath the old bed, she retrieved her lone duffel bag and put it on top of her faded yellow comforter. The duffel wasn't very big, but she and Nathan didn't have much. They had each other, and that was enough.

She yanked open the top drawer of the dresser. Scooping up an armful of Nathan's little undershirts, footed pajamas and socks, Juliet shoved the clothes unceremoniously into the duffel.

Harrison Rivers couldn't waltz in and lay claim to her child. Especially not for whatever price her own family naively decided on. Nor did he have any right to come back into her life and make her want things she now knew she could never have with him. He was worth *millions,* and she was worth, well, at the moment, not much.

Whatever had led him to deal with his grief by slipping his hand into hers that early summer day more than two years ago had apparently faded or he got over it or he came to his senses, or something.

The nasty little voice that camped out in her brain whispered, *The only thing that made him touch you back then was your willing smile.*

She stubbornly shook her head again as she packed the duffel. It hadn't been like that. They'd talked; they'd connected in a very profound way. They just hadn't talked much about things like names or jobs or inheritances.

Or futures.

She had foolishly allowed herself to live in the moment, to take a chance. To dream.

Now that dream of one day being with him again was being taken away from her by the realities of their lives. She didn't belong in his world, but she didn't belong in hers, either. She'd never had the guts to face that fact before. She'd never had the guts to face a lot of things.

Struggling to ward off a fresh torrent of tears, Juliet went back to the dresser. She and Nathan didn't need to stay here in her world. Not when her family couldn't see past their greed. With a hip to the bottom edge of the drawer to keep the broken front from falling to the floor, she pulled the second drawer open and emptied it of Nathan's overalls and sweats. She used the same hip to push the drawer closed.

Her reflection in the mirror above the dresser caught her attention. Nathan's bunny lamp gave off enough light that she could see a dirty handprint on her shoulder. Harrison was still leaving his mark on her.

She didn't want a man who popped into her life and made her believe in things that didn't exist. Like soul mates and knights in shining armor. She curled her lip at the thought. The guy just said he never wanted to love someone so much it cost him his control.

She and Nat would simply leave. She stuffed her armload into the bag. The two of them would go so far away no one would ever find them, no matter how rich he might be.

The thought of riches made Juliet pause before going back to the dresser to collect her few belongings. Instead, she knelt and pulled a large, dented, Dutch shortbread cookie tin from beneath the bed. Popping the lid open, she released a quiet sob and sat on her heels to stare at the white envelope resting on top of a battered, leather-bound volume of Shakespeare's works.

A faded Polaroid of her and her grandpa marked the page he'd been reading to her right before he died. Her grief hadn't allowed her to open the book since. Missing a loved one was probably the only thing besides Nathan she and Harrison had in common.

Looking at the envelope, she didn't need to pick it up and count how much money was inside. She knew exactly how much it held, exactly how much she'd managed to squirrel away since she'd convinced her mom to pay her minimum wage out of any profits the store made. Unfortunately, lately there rarely were any.

At one point she'd had close to five thousand dollars saved in that envelope. Five thousand dollars saved for college, for the school she'd been trying to screw up the courage to apply to.

Then she'd had Nat and had started dipping into the envelope to pay for things. Important things like the hospital, trips to the doctor, his crib and car seat. And that cute, fuzzy, blue snowsuit with bear ears that she'd bought when it had been so cold last winter. Juliet's gaze rose to the open duffel. And those overalls embroidered all over with little trains he loved so much. Important things like that.

Now her envelope contained exactly $249. They wouldn't get far on so little. Not far at all. Nat might even end up in danger. She'd rather die.

She slid her hand beneath the envelope to satisfy her ritual of tracing the tired lines of her grandfather's face peeking out above the book. Fresh tears streamed down her cheeks. Quietly she replaced the lid of the old cookie tin with a hollow snap.

Grandpa would have told her to fight for what was hers. He wouldn't have stood for this running-away nonsense, either. Grandpa would have gone toe-to-toe with anyone who'd tried to mess with his family. Shoot, he'd done as much when the state had made noises about taking her away from her own mother back when Mom couldn't declare which of her boyfriends had fathered Juliet. At least that's how he'd told the story.

No, Grandpa wouldn't want his granddaughter sitting on the floor crying because she didn't have enough money to run away. He'd want her to fight.

Since her grandpa was the only person Juliet had ever wanted to make proud, besides Nathan, of course, she shoved the round tin back beneath the bed and got to her feet. She would march herself downstairs and tell her no-good family again that she was the only one who had the right to decide anything about Nathan.

But after she eased closed the bedroom door behind her, a male voice reverberating up from the kitchen stopped her at the top of the stairs. Her hand turned to stone on the knob. She knew that voice in her heart as well as her head.

Harrison Rivers was downstairs, in her kitchen, talking to her greedy family.

The tremors that had seized her earlier in that very kitchen started once again, and she felt the blood leave her head. She couldn't face Harrison like this, with her eyes red and nose running. She didn't want him to think that she was weak and vulnerable. Not when he was the poster child for the confidence and self-assurance she had always wished she possessed.

But she had to know what he was saying to her family and, more important, what they were saying to him. So she started down the stairs.

Harrison's deep voice increased her shaking. "It wasn't my intention to upset Juliet."

"Don't you worry about that girl. She always did tend toward the emotional side," her mom said in a girlish, high-pitched voice reserved for men who caught her interest.

As if things weren't bad enough.

"Really." Harrison didn't sound particularly happy to hear the news.

Juliet scoffed. Wait until he tried to take Nat from her. Then he'd really see her emotional side.

"It's not like she's unstable or anything," she heard Willie offer.

Juliet moaned inwardly. Leave it to Willie to make things worse. She sank down on a stair, her knees too unsteady to support her.

Great. Just great. Plant words like *emotional* and *unstable* in Harrison's brain. Then he'd be chomping at the bit to rip Nathan from her arms at any cost.

She fisted her hands and forced herself back to her feet. She'd be damned if she'd cower in a dark stairway and let her family work up to portraying her as an unfit mother. That was one thing she was not. With renewed determination she descended the remaining stairs and turned the corner into the brightly lit kitchen.

At the sight of Harrison, she pulled up short not two steps into the room. While she had stopped a good yard from him, the breath left her as if she'd slammed into him at a dead run. She had never thought of their kitchen as big, but it had become absolutely tiny with him crowding the area. He completely filled the space between the table and the back door with his broad shoulders and tall frame. And he practically pulsated with an animal magnetism that made her break out in a very feminine sweat.

She hadn't noticed down by the river, but he still wore the clothes he had on earlier that day, and his white designer shirt and olive-colored pants looked as out of place next to the dingy linoleum and gold-speckled Formica as they had in the store. Only the strained look on his handsome face and finger-mussed, dark-gold hair kept him from looking like he'd just stepped out of his country club.

When he turned toward her and caught her gaze with his, Juliet couldn't regain the breath she'd lost. The look he gave her was far more wary than before, though just as intense. His wariness scared her, more than what her family had said. But as terrified as she was by what he might say or do, she couldn't tear her gaze from his, and the blood that had pooled in her feet at the first sound of his voice came surging back up through her body like a tempest.

Why did she feel so connected to him? So in tune that she swore she could feel his heartbeat throbbing through her from three feet away? Didn't her body know how dangerous he was to her? With a snap of his fingers he could take away her reason for living—Nathan. Not to mention what he could do to her heart. She forced herself to look away from his probing gaze.

"Well, speak of the devil," Willie piped up when he, too, caught sight of her from where he stood leaning against the fridge. "Sheesh, Julie, you look like you just ran one of those stupid marathons."

Juliet covered her flushed cheeks with her hands. It took a physical effort to cease gasping for air. She had to get ahold of herself or Harrison would easily believe what her family spouted about her mental health.

"Glad you decided to show, missy," her mom said from her permanent spot at the head of the small table. "Mr. Rivers, here, came to see his son."

She frowned at her mom. "*My* son is asleep."

Harrison held up a hand and shook his head. "I

don't expect you to wake him.'' He stepped around the table toward her, making a squishy sound with his shoe.

Juliet looked down and blinked when she saw his right leg was soaked from the ankle down. The cuff of his olive slacks and brown leather loafer were darkened with river water. She couldn't help but feel a small surge of empathy. There probably weren't any stagnant, ankle-deep puddles in front of his country club. He looked as uncomfortable and out of place in her world as she would in his.

He shifted again. She quickly looked up from his feet to his eyes when he continued, ''I also wanted to make sure you were all right.''

Juliet continued to helplessly return his stare. While concern showed plainly on his face, his initial wariness gave way to some other intense emotion swimming in the depths of his dark-green eyes. She was at a loss to name what she saw there. He looked different from when he'd been telling her about his mother's death. There'd been no mistaking the agony he felt then. Her own heart had answered in kind.

Whether he wanted to be or not, this was a man capable of deep feelings. And a true knight to his mother on her deathbed. But whatever motivation he had now, she wouldn't let him or her family sway her way of thinking.

Nathan was hers.

Even if her stupid body wanted to belong to Nathan's daddy.

Chapter Four

Harrison held his breath as he watched Juliet's lush brown eyes study him as if he was a Picasso. She looked horrified and intrigued all at once. She also looked like she'd been crying again.

Harrison silently swore to himself. Her pain touched him, affected him, the same way her pleasure had. Never in his life had a woman's passion so heightened his own. It was like she had somehow slipped under his skin with the first touch. He needed to either protect her in order to protect himself or learn to shut her out.

Unfortunately, neither would be easy.

"Are you all right?" he asked, repeating his question.

She let out an exasperated breath. "What do you think?"

"I think we need to talk," he stated firmly.

"Talk," her mom butted in. "Yes, that's what we need to do. We all need to sit down here and talk till we come up with an agreement that will resolve this little situation."

Juliet ground out, "Nathan is not a *situation*, Mom."

"He most certainly is, missy," her mother hissed. "And if you're not in the mood to cooperate, you can march yourself back up those stairs where you came from."

"Oh, so *now* you're going to start parenting me?"

Harrison interrupted before things got completely out of control. "I need to talk to Juliet. Alone." He reached a staying hand toward Juliet. She sidestepped away as though he'd offered her a snake. "I really drove up here tonight to see my...to see Nathan and to talk to Juliet. Just Juliet."

He pulled back his hand and took a step toward her. She swayed away but held her ground, her expression guarded. Again he marveled at her strength of will. And liked it a lot. Few people were willing to stand against him. It was a wonder her family hadn't broken her. The inane thought struck him that she was like a beautiful rosebud in a bouquet of milkweeds.

Patting down her extremely curly, dark-brown hair and practically batting her equally dark eyes at him, Juliet's mother said, "Well, as her mother, I feel it's only right that I do the negotiating—"

Harrison clenched his jaw to keep from gaping. Before he could restate his intentions, Juliet cut her mother off first.

"Negotiating?" she cried. "There isn't going to be any negotiating! Nathan isn't some used car you're trying to unload, he's my son. Mine! Not this...this guy's. He isn't Nat's father!"

Everyone spoke at once.

"Aw, get off it! What do you think we are? Retards?"

"Now, you look here, missy!"

"Juliet." Only Harrison's voice seemed to register with her, so he continued, "It's clear to me now that no one is going to decide anything at this moment. The situation is too overwhelming—for both of us— to try to change anything right off."

She looked away and crossed her arms in front of her full breasts, drawing his gaze despite his intentions. One more part of her he hadn't quite been able to forget. She had fit so perfectly in his hands his palms started to itch for want of the contact again.

"There's nothing to change. He isn't yours," she grumbled belligerently, drawing his attention from where it shouldn't be.

"Jeez, Jules," Willie groaned, and slapped a hand over his grubby, backward baseball hat. "What's with you? I can't believe you're going to let Natter miss out on havin' a guy like him for a dad."

Harrison narrowed his eyes on Willie. "What do you mean, 'a guy like me'?"

"Hell, just the fact you're standin' here screams *decent guy*. Most fellas would have turned tail and run the second they were given an out."

Harrison folded his arms over his chest. "I don't agree. I think most men want to be a part of their children's lives." Not to mention Juliet's. He nearly groaned. No. He didn't want to be a part of any woman's life right now, he reminded himself for the millionth time. He wanted to run his company and be a father to his son. End of story.

Willie laughed and shook his head. "Man, do you live in a soap opera, or what?"

Harrison turned the question on Willie. "Would *you* walk away from a child of your own?"

He didn't even take the time to think about his answer. "Like spit on ice."

It was Harrison's turn to shake his head. Not taking responsibility wasn't an option. "That shows how different we are."

Readjusting his shoulder against the refrigerator, Willie looked Harrison over from head to foot then started to chuckle. "You have no idea."

Remembering he was talking to the wrong person, Harrison turned back to the only one who mattered and uncrossed his arms. "Juliet, please. I told you before, I have every intention of being an integral part of Nathan's upbringing. I refuse to walk away from him."

Willie straightened up from the fridge. "Hey, a DNA test would prove you're the dad."

With a perplexed look her mother asked, "A what?"

Instantly recoiling from the thought of running blood tests on his baby, Harrison shook his head. "I don't think there's any need for clinically establishing paternity."

Willie made a noise and scratched his head through his baseball hat. To his mother he explained, "It's a test that would show Nat's his. You know, like those spit tests they use on *AMW*."

Harrison frowned. "*AMW?*"

Willie gave him appalled look. "*America's Most Wanted.* Man, you really are out there."

Visibly paled, Juliet insisted, "I won't agree to it."

"You might not have a choice, Jules."

Tired of the interference, Harrison sent her brother a look that made him hunker down into the nearest chair.

In a much less harsh tone her mother said, "Stop fighting it, Julie. If you think for a second, you'll know this is for the best."

Maybe the woman did care a little for Juliet's feelings.

Juliet sniffed and threw out a hip. "You didn't stop fighting when you were in my shoes."

"That was your grandpa's doing. I would have gladly let the state take you. I had my hands full already with your brother, here."

Harrison sucked in a breath at the older woman's cruel words. So much for caring for Juliet's feelings.

"Well, it's a good thing I'm more like Grandpa than you, now, isn't it?" Juliet said, her pain so clear on her face he wanted to gather her in his arms and make everything better.

She glanced at him, and he willed her to understand that he wasn't the enemy. It didn't work. She raised her chin in defiance. While he admired her tenacity, her refusal to cooperate was wearing thin.

"Don't you worry none about her," Willie offered. "If we need proof Natter's yours, I'll make sure you get it."

"Willie!" Juliet gave her brother a horrified look.

"If anyone can do it, Willie can," Juliet's mother said with a permed nod, not even batting an eye at betraying her daughter. "They're real close."

Harrison could barely suppress a snort. He doubted either of them knew a thing about Juliet. And if he wanted to convince her to move to his estate, he knew he'd have to find a way to get close to her, himself. Looking at her mother and brother, he said, "I think this is something that Juliet and I should work through together. Alone."

Without giving her time to protest, Harrison took Juliet's hand and pulled her into the dim store.

The way her hand fit so perfectly within his registered in his brain and the need to gather her in his arms nearly overwhelmed him. But he hardened his heart with determination. They would end this nonsense and they would end it now.

He rounded on her. "You realize, don't you, that I can find a way to prove Nathan is mine? Your family is more than willing to offer him up to me."

"He isn't theirs to—"

"And you won't admit he's mine, either. That leaves me with only one choice. Do you really want to put Nathan through a paternity test?"

While he wasn't exactly sure how the procedure was performed, just the thought of willfully putting his little boy through any sort of pain or discomfort made his chest very, very tight. Since he had no intention of ever letting his son be hurt, he had to convince Juliet that he knew what he was talking about.

He put his hands on his hips and leaned toward her. "It's *not* some spit test, you know. Nor will they simply prick his heel or finger. They'll use a needle."

The possibility made his heart constrict until he had to force the words out. "They'll stick a needle into our baby's tiny arm, into his delicate, unsuspecting skin, and take vials of his blood. *Vials.* Just in case they have to run duplicate tests if one of us appeals, you know. All because you won't admit I'm his father. Why, Juliet? Why won't you admit that I'm the only man you've ever been with?"

Her brown-and-gold eyes went wide and shimmered as though he'd been peeking in her diary.

The spark of possessiveness she'd ignited in him

roared to life like a fire caught in a backdraft. "I haven't forgotten that I was your first," he whispered thickly. "I know in my gut that what Willie says about you is true, that you haven't let another man near you." He raised a hand and skimmed her soft cheek with his knuckles. "It's true, isn't it?"

Her nod was so slight he would have missed it if he hadn't been touching her face.

"For Nathan's sake, admit I'm his father."

Juliet's heart lodged in her throat and nearly strangled her. She struggled to ignore the torturous pleasure the simple touch of his fingers on her cheek sent through her and stared hard into his mossy eyes, appearing black in the dim light. Try as she may, she couldn't find the sort of underhandedness a corporate bigwig like him must be capable of. All she saw was the truth in his words.

He was right. She couldn't bear to have Nathan deliberately hurt. No matter the cost to herself. With pain, her family's betrayal, and anger at her own foolishness heating her face, she turned away from him. Away from his touch and the pleasure she didn't want to feel. "Okay, I admit it," she whispered. "You're Nathan's father."

"Thank you." His gratitude sounded heartfelt.

She couldn't meet his eyes. She didn't want to see the gloating or thrill of victory where she had once seen the promise of something wonderful.

His deep voice washed over her in the near darkness, drowning her. "I suppose I should go for now. We can talk some more tomorrow."

She shrugged noncommittally. Seeing how she had just laid down her last weapon against him, it didn't matter. She was as good as road kill beneath the wheels of her dream on a bike.

As HARRISON WENT to his car, he didn't feel the elation or thrill of victory he'd expected to feel once he convinced Juliet to tell the truth. Rather than climbing in right away, he stood for a moment, his elbows propped on his Porsche's roof, and stared out across the highway to where he knew the river flowed.

What he did feel was the quiet, calm certainty of having done the right thing. Being the best father he could possibly be to his son was definitely the right thing. And helping Juliet along the way wouldn't be a bad thing, either. A little atonement could do a lot of good.

Now all he had to do was convince her that moving to the Rivers estate was not only the right thing but the only thing to do.

He unlocked the driver's door and was opening it when Juliet's mother hailed him from the rickety little balcony.

"Oh, Harrison," she called in a molar-grinding falsetto. "Your *son* is awake and has convinced his mother he needs a snack. I'm sure Juliet wouldn't mind if you joined them."

Knowing darn well she *would* mind, he hesitated.

Her mother rushed to add, "It'll just be the two of you. I need my beauty sleep, and Willie's shows are on. I thought you might like to spend a bit more time with *your son*." She said the words like they were the magic ones.

They were.

He slammed his car door shut and started toward

the store. ''Yes, I would,'' he said, then went into the store.

He passed through the dark living room just as Willie switched on the television, and Harrison noted once again the clutter consuming the place. The door to the brighter kitchen was bracketed by twin, waist-high stacks of old newspapers he hadn't noticed before. Apparently recycling trucks didn't come this far up the river road. Or maybe no one ever set the papers out.

Either way, he couldn't help but narrow his eyes a little more. While he knew Juliet's life would be turned upside down, he was growing more and more convinced that she and their baby couldn't continue living like this.

Their baby.

Those unspoken words sent the now familiar, intense surge of possessiveness through him. He wouldn't allow her to push him away. He'd convince her to let him take her home with him where he could care for them both. Then everything would be right with his world again because he would be back in control.

A loud sniff brought his attention to the kitchen, and he stepped into the room. Juliet sat at the table, squirting great globs of Cheez Whiz on crackers to the immense delight of their toddler on her lap. Harrison watched for a moment in fascination, having never actually seen the orange stuff before.

As if sensing his presence, her gaze jumped to his and her expression turned guarded. ''Why are you still here?'' She handed Nathan a freshly topped cracker which he promptly began to strip of the cheese with his little tongue.

In a soft, nonthreatening voice Harrison replied, "Your mother caught me as I was leaving and said Nathan was up. She thought I might want to spend a little time with him tonight." He took a step toward the table. "I do."

She gave a mirthless laugh. "And here I was thinking you'd decided to demand I hand over your son to you right now." She gripped Nathan tightly to her, belying the sarcasm in her tone.

Harrison moved to stand in front of the table, struggling to dispel the image of the newspaper stacks from his mind. "Why would you think I'd do something like that?" What had he done to make her distrust him so? *Besides never coming back to see her and threatening her with tests.* Guilt and regret pricked at him in a way a needle never could. But coming back right after that first time wouldn't have solved anything. She would have still been pregnant, their lives still irrevocably changed.

"Why would I—" she started, then sputtered, "Because you're a bazillionaire and I'm...I'm—"

"White trash," Willie casually supplied for her from the doorway behind Harrison.

Juliet's face turned crimson. "I am not," she denied throatily.

Willie chuckled. "Well, you sure as heck ain't no deb."

Harrison slowly turned to him, on the brink of doing her brother serious damage. "Would you mind giving us some privacy?" he grated out, balling his hands into fists at his sides. One of these days he was going to have to hit his baby's uncle.

Willie innocently raised both brows, then nodded. "Oh. Sure, sure. No problem. I just need to get a brewsky, then I'll leave you two kids alone.'' He sauntered over to the refrigerator and retrieved a can of beer, then headed back toward the living room. ''I'll be in here watching the tube if you need me.'' He saluted them with the silver can and disappeared through the door.

Harrison turned back to Juliet. The expression on her face drew him to the chair closest to her. He wouldn't have thought someone could look any more hurt than she had when Willie and her mother had supported doing the paternity test, but the look she wore now spoke of a much deeper sorrow.

''Juliet,'' he softly entreated, but she ignored him by studiously replenishing the Cheez Whiz on the cracker Nathan had licked clean and held out for her with a noisy, incomprehensible demand. The trembling of her hands made Harrison's chest unbearably tight.

He instinctively reached out and covered her hand. Her skin was icy cold. God, how he wanted to hold her and warm her. Just the thought of her in his arms raised his own temperature and brought his body to life. ''Juliet, I'm sure I don't have to tell you that your brother is a jerk.''

She shrugged as if it didn't matter, but her chin began to tremble, too.

''You are not—'' he couldn't make himself say the reprehensible words that so clearly hurt her ''—any of the things Willie says. You are a strong, courageous, beautiful woman who has done the best she could considering—'' he glanced at Nathan's sweet face then at the cracked glass of the kitchen window ''—your circumstances.''

Her lifestyle was so different from his. But would

her reaction to his reappearance in her life have been any different if she had grown up with the same privileges he had—if she were wealthy, too? Would she have touched him so deeply?

He pulled in a breath and forced himself to be honest. The answer was, *Probably not.* Because she wouldn't have been the same person. She wouldn't have been able to show him the simple peace of life when he'd so desperately needed it. Though, he knew without a doubt that no matter where he encountered her, his body would always want her. The electricity that sparked between them was undeniable. Too bad it *had* to be denied.

He fixed his gaze on her again, but she still wouldn't look at him. ''You know, there's nothing all that great about being a debutante, either.''

''I...'' She stopped to clear her throat, keeping her attention on Nathan. ''I imagine you would know a lot about debutantes. Just like I'm sure you know a lot about fancy tests. And *lawyers.*'' Her voice shook nearly as much as her hands.

Harrison felt consumed with remorse. He wanted so much to have her trust back. She had trusted him infinitely that day two years ago. So much so she'd given herself completely to him. Insanely, he wanted to see the warm glow back in her beautiful brown-gold eyes. No one had ever looked at him like she had, before or since. She had made him feel like there was nothing he couldn't do, nothing he couldn't handle. She had freed him of his burdens with a simple touch of her hand and the welcoming fire of her body. His own tightened and throbbed at the memory.

Shaking the memories off, he squeezed her hand. ''You don't have to be afraid of me, Juliet.''

"You've probably dated a ton of debutantes, haven't you?"

"That would be an exaggeration." He hadn't dated at all since his mother's death.

"But you know some, right?"

She tried to pull her hand from beneath his. He wouldn't let her. She wasn't going to push him away this time. For some inexplicable reason he wanted to find that place they had shared when they'd first met, if only for a moment. He wanted her to look at him without judgment or speculation again. He started rubbing the pad of his thumb over the satiny skin on the back of her hand, taking wicked pleasure in the way she shifted in her seat. Nathan responded by rocking back and forth and humming while he ate.

The fact that she had asked him something finally registered. "Some what?"

She glanced up at him, her expression telling him exactly what she thought of his mental capabilities. "Debutantes. You know some debutantes, don't you?"

"Oh. Yes, I suppose. My sister, Ashley, was one. That's how I know it's not so great."

Juliet drew her finely arched brows together. "She didn't like it?"

He scratched his emerging beard with his free hand. "Well, actually, Ashley loved it. But that's Ashley. She's into that sort of thing. I personally thought what she had to go through—the parties, the virtual stock shows—was rather degrading."

She rolled her eyes. "Gee, parties. How awful." Then her mouth and delicate brow tightened. "I'm sure she was more than a little surprised to find out you'd gone slumming."

He squeezed her hand harder, then slipped his thumb beneath her hand so he could stroke her palm. He found her skin moist there. "I did *not* go slumming. I was...searching for...something."

She looked at him, her expression unreadable but for the fierceness in her glittering eyes. "And you found me."

The possessiveness and his physical need for her surged again. He pulled her hand toward him. "Yes. I found you."

"Lucky me."

He nearly flinched from her sarcasm, but stared hard into her eyes, willing her to understand. "But now I'm back, ready to be a father to our son. And I *am* his father." He needed her to reiterate her earlier declaration, to make sure she hadn't changed her mind.

"Yes. You are," she said with what Harrison at first thought was a wistful tone, but decided it must have been resignation.

Her acceptance of the situation was exactly what he needed to regain control of himself. He let go of her hand and leaned back, releasing a noisy breath. "Good. I'm glad we have that settled." He looked to his son on her lap. The little guy was covered from ear to ear with Cheez Whiz. Harrison smiled and reached a finger to wipe a glob off Nathan's cheek, then tasted it. "Hmm. Not bad. Does he ever actually eat the crackers?"

"Sometimes." She smiled back, relaxing the rigidity of her back a bit. "Mostly he just likes to lick the cheese off."

Nathan confirmed his preference by chanting, "'Eeze, 'eeze, 'eeze."

Harrison leaned forward again. "I'd love to learn what else he likes. Will you let me?"

"Do I have a choice?"

"Damn it, Juliet—"

She held up a hand to stop his tirade before he could get started. "All right. I'm sorry. And watch your language around you-know-who."

Harrison took another deep breath to loosen the vise grip that seized his gut the second she'd made him think they had taken three steps backward toward hostility. "Of course."

He watched them for a moment, his heart swelling with an intense sort of satisfaction he'd never experienced before, not even in the boardroom. He reached out and smoothed the brow Nathan had raised at his outburst. Nathan handed him a slobbery cracker, and his heart nearly exploded.

Despite how much he wanted them out of this place, Harrison knew he still needed to tread carefully. After the upset of today, tomorrow would definitely be soon enough to ask her to move to the estate. "Can I see you two tomorrow?"

"*See* us tomorrow?" she squeaked. "I figured you'd just call when you said we'd talk tomorrow. Don't you have a megacorporation to run?"

Harrison shifted in the too-small seat. He didn't want to scare her off by talking about his world, but he knew he needed to gain a small measure of her trust by opening up to her. "Yes, I do. Sort of."

"What do you mean *sort of*? Willie's friend said you'd taken over for your dad."

"He's still CEO and chairman of the board. I'm only president."

"*Only* president." She laughed softly, flashing her straight, white teeth.

He responded instantly with an irrational amount of pleasure. Damn, but she was beautiful. Sitting there with wind-tousled hair and not a bit of makeup, she was the very embodiment of natural beauty. She didn't need Coco Chanel or pearls to look good. All she had to do was be.

Suddenly an image of Juliet lying naked on a moss-softened rock down by the water flashed in his brain. He could imagine how the river's breath would gently lift her long hair and tighten her breasts like his hands would. Her sighs of pleasure would mingle with the sounds of the river just as her tears had.

The thought of her tears, and the fact that he had caused them, snapped him out of the fantasy like a slap to the face.

He cleared his throat and focused again on explaining his father to her. "He's going to retire soon, so it won't be long before I really will have an entire megacorporation to run."

She rested her chin atop Nathan's head, a curious look in her gold-flecked eyes. "Aren't you nervous about being totally in charge of so much?"

Having been asked the same question numerous times by members of the board, what was now his stock answer came quickly. "Not at all. Since I've been president I have never made a mistake. My judgment is sound. I can handle the company on my own."

"Never said you couldn't," she softly assured him.

Harrison tried to stem the tension creeping up the back of his neck by rubbing it. The opposition to his plans for the Dover Creek Mill was really getting to him, despite his best efforts. "Then you're one of a few. Apparently the members of the board don't think I'm old enough or 'tempered' enough to be in charge."

"Then you'll just have to prove them wrong," she said with quiet confidence.

Nathan babbled something around a cracker that sounded an awful lot like concurrence.

Harrison refused to acknowledge the warmth that flooded through him because of her faith in his abilities. It was one thing to be flooded by the heat of desire, but to need her approval would make him as vulnerable as his father had been. He couldn't let that happen.

"Is your dad that old? I mean, retirement age?"

"No, he's not. Not at all. But he hasn't been the same since my mom died. He needs to go off and find something that will make him happy again."

She lifted her chin from Nathan's head and sat back in her seat. "Like you did?"

He looked away, wishing he'd phrased his dad's reasons for retiring differently. But Harrison's time with Juliet *had* allowed him to return to his life, to get past his grief. Yet wanting to downplay the importance of that time and his vulnerability where she was concerned, he gave a slight shrug. "I guess."

An uncomfortable awareness crackled between them. She had to be thinking of how he had practically clung to her after they had made love, unwilling to release her from his embrace and sacrifice the haven he'd found in her. Then Nathan reached up and stuck a goopy finger in her ear with a squeal of delight and distracted her from whatever she might have been reliving.

Despite the additional surge of warmth her laugh at their son's antics sent through him, he vowed to prove to her that he didn't need that haven anymore. He might *want* to have her in his arms, but he didn't *need* her. He simply wanted to make her life better for Nathan's sake. Lust could be controlled, he reminded himself.

Harrison decided it was time to get back to the subject at hand. "So...I'll come back tomorrow." When she hesitated, he compromised as much as he was willing to and added. "I'll call first."

"Tomorrow," she agreed in a near whisper. "But we'll have to figure out a schedule. Schedules are very important to toddlers."

"Schedules are a very good thing," he agreed, his heart soaring. He'd have them out of here before the end of the week. He'd known she would be reasonable if they had a chance to talk. "I also promise to always have you two back here in time for his nap or bedtime—whichever applies."

She frowned again, her hand stilling in the process of wiping the gooey mess from Nathan's face. "What do you mean, have us back? You aren't taking us anywhere."

Harrison placed his hands on the table and forced himself to stay calm. "I assumed I would take you—both of you—home to meet my family, to play at my house."

Suspicion rolled off her in waves. "Why?"

"So you and Nathan can get to know me and my family, see where and how I live." He tried to sound casual, but getting her home to see how much better her life could be at the estate was critical to convincing her to move there.

"No." She pushed her chair back, its metal legs scraping on the floor, and stood. Hoisting Nathan onto her hip, she pronounced, "You can visit Nathan, and get to know him, but he's not stepping a foot into your house."

Harrison sat back in his chair and unconsciously assumed his best boardroom pose, arms stretched to their full length with his hands spread on the table. His first instinct was to get angry with her for being uncooperative again. But he rationalized that as long as he got to spend time with her, she'd get to know him and see that he would be a good, responsible influence on their son. Then she would allow him to improve both their lives by moving them out of this place.

And maybe, just maybe, he'd discover why she pulled at him, why she'd haunted him for over two damn years. Then he would be able to put an end to it.

He raised a hand and slapped it back down on the table. "Agreed." Mentally adding, *For now*.

Nathan smiled at the noise and leaned forward in his mother's arms in an attempt to slap the table himself.

Juliet's jaw visibly tightened as if she was fighting to keep it from dropping. Clearly she'd expected Harrison to balk at the idea.

Think again, sweetheart.

He rose from the table and stepped toward Juliet to tweak their son's nose. "I'll see you soon, Nat. You be a good boy for your mamma."

"Liclic!" Nathan squealed and pointed a cheesy finger at Harrison's pant leg.

Harrison glanced at his slacks and grinned when he

saw the faint, reddish stain left by his first encounter with his son. "He remembers getting his licorice stuck on my leg. Do you have some in the store I could buy for him?"

Juliet shook her head decisively. "He's had enough sweets today. He needs to go back to bed."

With a disappointed sigh for missing an opportunity to bond with his son, he looked into Nathan's hopeful, dark-green eyes. "Sorry, buddy. Daddy's clean out of licorice."

"Dada liclic," Nathan pleaded, reaching his little arms to Harrison.

His eyes burning and his throat tight, Harrison reached for his son.

Juliet held him fast to her chest, her eyes huge with dread.

Certain that his time with his son would come, Harrison chucked him on his tiny cleft chin. "Next time, little man. Next time." Looking to Juliet, he smiled gently. "Don't worry. Everything will be fine."

But as Harrison walked out through the disorganized living room, he noticed Willie asleep atop a pile of laundry dumped on the couch. He continued through the tidier but sorely understocked store and became certain there was only one way everything would ever be fine with him.

He had to bring Nathan and Juliet home with him for good. And quick.

Chapter Five

She'd admitted it.

She'd admitted Harrison Rivers was Nathan's father. The words had actually left her mouth after she'd vowed they never would. Juliet couldn't help but wonder what other vows she'd break now that Harrison was a part of her life.

She tried not to think about what she'd done. She really did. But Nathan's chant of "Dada liclic, Dada liclic," while she washed the cheese and crackers off him and readied him for bed again made it impossible. She squeezed her little boy to her chest one last time before laying him back down in his crib.

Pulling the quilt over Nathan, she responded by rote with a "Yes night-night" to each of his yawned "No night-night."

Not only had she admitted what she'd sworn she wouldn't, she'd agreed to let Harrison visit. To get to know Nathan. To fall in love with Nathan. And her baby would fall for Harrison. He might even come to love his father more than he loved her.

She squeezed her eyes tight against the pain in her heart, thinking of the way Harrison's rumbling laugh, gentle touch and warm eyes had reached inside and

touched her. Two years ago he had made her feel
special and important within five minutes of meeting
him. And he'd done it again tonight when he'd placed
her feelings and opinions above those of her family.

Yeah, her baby would fall in love with his father.
He wouldn't be able to help himself. Just as she
hadn't been able to help herself.

Maybe if she stayed close she could minimize the
damage. And she'd be spending time with Harrison.
Juliet pushed the thought away. She refused to go
down that road. She'd fought so hard to bury her feelings for the man who had roared into her life for a
few glorious hours, and she wasn't about to let them
worm their way to the surface now. Not when she
could never have a place in his life as anything but
Nathan's mother.

No, she'd stay close to father and son and make
sure Harrison didn't try to make Nathan want to leave
her to live with him.

An oppressive, smothering weight settled on her
chest. It was the same feeling she'd had when Willie
had held her underwater while they were swimming
in the river one summer. She would drown without
Nathan in her life.

The need to cling to him like a life preserver made
her reach into the crib and pick up the drowsy toddler
again. Thankfully, he didn't squirm in protest when
she pulled him tight to her chest. Maybe he understood how much she needed him. And maybe, just
maybe, she could make Harrison understand, too.

THE CRACKED, UNEVEN CEMENT burned the bottoms
of Juliet's feet. She should have put shoes on. Shoot.
Barefoot and "ignant," that's how they'd see her. But

she didn't want to run in and grab her shoes and risk
their visitors showing up and coming in before she
could stop them.

Lord, what had she been thinking agreeing to his
coming today? And it wouldn't be just Harrison. He'd
said that since she wouldn't go to meet them, he was
bringing his family to meet her and Nat.

His family. Great. Since hanging up the phone this
morning all she could imagine was a line of luxury
sedans—no, *limos*—pulling off the highway, filled
with Kennedy wannabes who would refuse to sit on
her furniture for fear of being "soiled." That's why
she stood out in front of the store, roasting in the early
September sun, instead of waiting inside. She didn't
want them to see the inside. The outside of the place
was bad enough.

She risked a glance away from the highway to
check on Nathan playing beneath the willow tree at
the corner of the store. Heaven forbid he would actually sit on the huge blue blanket she'd spread out
in the shade. But the fact that she wanted him clean
and looking nice naturally meant he'd find the first
chance to sit in the dirt. Man. Barefoot, "ignant,"
and *dirty*. That's how they would see her and Nathan.

She looked back to the highway and mentally
gauged how long it would take her to run upstairs and
grab her Keds. Her *guests* would probably pick that
moment to show up and see Nat sitting out here by
himself. She'd purposefully scheduled this visit for
when her mom went to town, and she'd convinced
Willie to go help his friend Dave work on his car. If
Harrison's family arrived while she was inside they'd
think she was a bad mother.

Of course, then she would only be "ignant," dirty and inattentive, because she'd have her shoes on.

The decision was made for her, though, when a black Mercedes sedan appeared within view. It had to be Harrison. Juliet held her breath, but no limousines followed him into the parking lot.

Not so much as a Caddie.

Hope soared within her. Maybe his family hadn't wanted to meet the heir apparent's mistake.

That hope crashed and her cheeks flamed when she saw more than one head inside the car. But instead of the brimming carload she expected, only two other people had come with Harrison. Two women from what she could tell. One of them was probably his debutante sister coming for a look-see, Juliet thought sourly.

When Harrison brought the car to a stop in front of her, she could see that the person in the passenger seat had gray hair, and a blonde sat in back. While clearly different in ages, both women were equally well coifed, sporting stylish, blunt cuts. Harrison's debutante sister and grandmother?

A touch of relief cooled Juliet's cheeks. Maybe his sister would be too self-absorbed and his grandma too doddering to realize Juliet and Harrison's relationship wasn't exactly noble and romantic.

The car doors swung open and Harrison, wearing a beige, long-sleeved polo shirt and black pants, met her gaze with warm, smiling eyes as he got out.

Juliet's cheeks flared again.

He really looked happy to be here, as though he couldn't wait to introduce their son to the women preparing to climb from the other side of the car.

"Hello, there," Harrison said in his rich, deep

voice. "I see you're as anxious to show off Nathan as I am." He put words to her thoughts and smiled as he went around the front of the car to offer his help to the older woman.

"Yeah, right," Juliet mumbled.

Tucking the hand of the strikingly beautiful older woman in the crook of his arm, he escorted her around the car as she smoothed the wrinkles from her navy-blue silk pantsuit with her other hand. The woman Juliet assumed to be his sister, equally beautiful and looking like something straight from a Ralph Lauren catalog in chinos and yellow silk blouse with a matching scarf, hung back. "And I can't think of anyone I'd rather show him off to first than my favorite grandmother."

"I'm your only grandmother now, darling," the older woman chided, her voice as rich and smooth as her grandson's.

Juliet looked into the sharp, dark-green gaze of the petite, well-preserved old lady, and the heat in her cheeks grew hotter. This woman knew. She knew the whole story.

A sinking feeling pulled at Juliet's belly. How could she talk to his grandmother knowing the woman would be judging her? The people in Juliet's world were aware that she had only been with a man once, but Harrison's family didn't know it.

Harrison himself claimed to believe it, though, and his faith gave her the courage to stand her ground, hot cheeks, bare feet and all.

But the quick, subtle once-over his grandma gave Juliet as she approached her appeared more curious than judgmental.

Harrison slipped his grandma's thin, veined hand,

the only place she really showed her age, from his arm into his own. "Grandmother, I'd like you to meet Juliet Jones. Juliet, this is my grandmother, Dorothy Rivers."

Dorothy reached for Juliet's hand with her free one, her grip warm and surprisingly strong. "It's a pleasure, Miss Jones." Although she said it like she meant it, Juliet doubted she did.

"Considering...everything," Juliet left the obvious and embarrassing unsaid, "you should call me Juliet. Or Julie, if you'd like."

Dorothy slid her hand from Juliet's and cleared her throat as if uncomfortable with the blatant reminder of the circumstances of their acquaintance. Juliet shoved her hands in the front pockets of her jeans and glanced at Harrison.

He returned her gaze and smiled softly. "No, not Julie. Juliet."

The rock that had settled in her gut lightened somewhat. He could make her feel better with so little effort. She didn't dare think what it would be like to have him really try to make her feel good.

Seeming to recover from her lapse in manners, Dorothy reached back out and patted Juliet's arm. "That's a beautiful and fitting name, my dear."

Juliet shuffled her feet, then wished she hadn't when it reminded her they were bare. "Thank you," she murmured, and hoped no one looked down.

The younger woman stepped forward with a proffered hand. "And you can call me Ashley. I'm Harrison's sister." She flashed a stunningly perfect smile as she shook Juliet's hand and gave her the once-over as smoothly as her grandmother had, only she did a bad job of hiding the curiosity in her blue-green eyes.

Juliet certainly didn't have to guess where this woman's interest came from. Ashley was probably dying to know what Juliet had that would make Harrison cross the tracks and dip his privileged self in such a shallow gene pool. She also probably couldn't wait to catch a glimpse of whatever moral deficiency Juliet had that made her willing to get it on with a guy she hadn't known.

Juliet looked back to Harrison and admitted that, to the casual observer, his looks alone could easily be blamed for what had happened. A man as compelling as Harrison should be kept under lock and key. Any guy who could reduce a girl to mush just by running his big, warm hand up the nape of her neck and whispering how beautiful he thought she was shouldn't be allowed out into the general population.

Juliet raised her arm to shadow her eyes and cover her heated cheeks as she looked back at the two women. "It's nice to meet you."

Nathan saved her from having to come up with anything else by squealing, "Mama!" and throwing a fistful of dirt into the air. He giggled in delight when the grime fell onto his once-clean pant legs.

"Oh," Dorothy breathed softly and grabbed Harrison's sleeve. Her expression held so much excitement and joy the gentle lines on her face virtually disappeared. "Is that him?"

"Yes, Grandmother. That's my son," Harrison answered thickly, pride dripping from every word.

Juliet felt her heart start to come apart in her chest.

Dorothy released her grandson's sleeve and brought her hand up to her pale cheek. "Ohh. Oh, my, oh, my. You were so right, Harrison. He's beautiful. Absolutely beautiful." And as if Nathan sang a

Siren's song, the grand dame of the Rivers family moved toward him. She stopped a few feet from the seated toddler, stretching both hands down to him like one of the wise men at the Nativity.

Nathan responded by placing a small fistful of soil mined from the base of the tree into one of her open hands and uttered something close to "dirt."

Juliet started to groan, but stopped at the sound of Harrison's grandmother's delighted giggle.

"Why, thank you," she cooed to the child. "Yes, it is dirt, isn't it?" Dorothy Rivers glanced back over her shoulder at them, her eyes misty with emotion. "He's sharing with me." Turning back to Nathan, she stated knowingly, "And such good dirt, too. Just right for throwing *up in the air*," she sing-songed and tossed her handful straight up in the air. Both child and great-grandmother shrieked their pleasure as the dirt rained down on them.

Juliet's jaw dropped. Dirt throwing? That was absolutely, positively, the last thing she would have expected.

"What a cutie," Ashley said, and went to join the laughing pair under the tree. Her silk blouse and jauntily tied scarf didn't stand a chance.

Harrison's deep chuckle brought Juliet's attention to him. She snapped her mouth shut at the sight of his handsome face made even more gorgeous by his expression. His sensuous mouth sported a wide grin that showed all his straight, white teeth, and his full-lashed eyes crinkled adorably at the corners. Arms crossed over his big chest, he rocked back on his heels in amusement like a well-pleased king.

As if sensing she was looking at him, he said, "I

knew she'd be great with him, I just didn't know she'd be *that* great.''

Juliet looked back to her son and his great-grandmother and gasped when she saw that the woman had dropped down on her knees next to the toddler and was scooping up fresh handfuls of dirt.

''Oh, jeez,'' Juliet moaned and rushed toward them, thinking Harrison's grandmother would later regret her impulsiveness when she realized she'd ruined her expensive suit.

''Mrs. Rivers, please, this blanket is clean if you'd like to sit here.'' Juliet snatched up the edge of the pilled, blue blanket and started to pull it toward the older woman. ''Or if you'd like, I could run inside and get you a chair?''

She waved Juliet off with a grubby hand. ''No, no, dear. I'm fine right here. And please, call me Dorothy.''

The afternoon sun glinting off the large diamond ring Mrs. Rivers wore on her aged finger caught Juliet's gaze. The clean brilliance of it defied the film of dust and stood out against the brown dirt on her knuckles. A now-familiar tightness seized Juliet's chest at the reminder of how different she and Nathan were from Harrison and his family. No matter how down and dirty they got, the Riverses would always be rich and cultured and privileged and she and her baby were…well, they weren't any of those things.

She took a deep breath to loosen the squeeze reality always put on her insides. ''But your beautiful suit…it'll be ruined.''

''Oh, pish. What's a little dirt?'' Dorothy looked up at Juliet and paused, mid dirt toss, to consider her for a moment. ''Besides,'' she continued gently, "getting to know this little angel on his terms is far, far more important than this old wad of fabric and thread." She glanced from Ashley to Harrison, who had wandered over to join them. The three exchanged a silent look that had Juliet nervously shifting her weight on her bare feet again.

Did they think she cared more about clothes than making her child happy? Juliet gritted her teeth and wished, for the millionth time, that life had a rewind button.

"Harrison," Dorothy finally addressed her grandson. "Why don't you take Juliet for a long walk and let Ashley and me have some aunt and great-grandma time. That is," Dorothy looked back to Juliet, "if it's acceptable to Juliet."

All sorts of alarm bells went off in Juliet's head, but while she tried to figure out if leaving Nathan alone with the Rivers women was worse than her going off alone with Harrison, he answered for her.

"I suppose that would be fine. Clearly he isn't going to give me a second look with turbo great-grandma here to entertain him."

"And me," Ashley interjected, crouching down next to Nathan. "I'm sure Aunt Ashley can scare up some real ants for us to play with."

"Bugs!" Nathan shouted in delight.

Ashley wrinkled her perfect nose and tweaked Nathan on his tiny one. "That's right. We'll find us some great big bugs."

Harrison laughed and turned to Juliet and offered her one of his large, strong hands.

Staring at it, she stammered, "I...I...don't think—"

"Come on." He took a step and grabbed her hand,

his warm fingers threading through hers. "Just for a little bit. Don't worry," he reassured her, looking deep into her eyes and reeling her heart in like a fish on a hook. He tried to pull her forward, his expression screaming *trust me.*

Juliet pulled back on his hand and dug in her bare heels, knowing she didn't dare. His mere presence affected her so deeply her heart would never survive his focused attention.

But Nathan glanced up at her and waved. "Bye-bye, Mommy. Bye—bye."

"See?" Harrison whispered. "It'll be okay. Come on."

Juliet relented and let him pull her toward the road, feeling helpless against the tide of change and uncertainty swirling around her. "I thought you wanted to get to know Nathan," she said, picking her way over the sharp gravel.

"I do," he threw over his shoulder. "But I have more time than Grandmother does."

"What?" Juliet yanked on his hand to stop him. She looked back at the woman drawing in the dirt with Nathan as Ashley poked at the tree for bugs. While she didn't look ill, Juliet knew Dorothy Rivers had to be pretty old and could have all sorts of health problems.

"No, no. She's not dying or anything," he correctly guessed her train of thought. "At least not anytime soon. She's as healthy as a horse. She routinely creams me in golf."

When she turned back to him, he grinned that grin at her. The one that had lured her off the balcony in the first place. Her temperature shot up a few thousand degrees.

Obnoxiously oblivious to his effect on her, he continued, "But she doesn't drive much anymore, and she runs about a dozen charities, so it'll be more difficult for her to get up here to visit than for me."

"Yeah, because all you have to do is prove you can run a multimillion-dollar company."

His grin faded. He turned and headed them toward the river again. "Don't worry," he repeated, and checked the highway in both directions. "I'll have plenty of time to get to know Nathan as well as you do." He darted across the road, pulling her along at a run behind him.

She really hated when he said things like that. He sounded way too much like a father planning on living with his son. Of course, he wouldn't have hauled his beloved grandma and sister up here if he intended to take Nathan away from her, would he?

She looked up from the ground to watch the way the muscles in his broad back moved beneath his beige polo shirt. She remembered how those muscles had felt beneath her fingertips. Smooth and hard. She had trusted him so completely that day two years ago.

She wanted desperately to trust him now, to believe he wasn't lying to her and that he wouldn't take Nat away from her. And he might not. But could she really bear to have him visit every weekend with the memory of his fingertips on her body? Thinking about how his hot breath had felt when he'd buried his face in the crook of her neck and arched his strong back to ease into her, filling both her body and soul?

Juliet stumbled down the path to the riverbed. Only Harrison's firm grip on her hand kept her from crashing headfirst onto the rocks separating the river from the trees and bushes growing on the slope below the road.

"Whoa, there," he laughed, reaching his other hand to catch her waist and bring her up against him to stop her fall.

With images of their lovemaking vivid in her mind and his body pressed against hers, Juliet's knees refused to support her.

He affected her exactly the same now as that first time. Every inch of him was electric, thrilling her where they touched. And his eyes, so like the river flowing silently beside them, pulled her in, lured her away from her convictions with the promise of pleasure and security.

She didn't know how long she leaned against him, staring into the bottomless depths of his eyes, but when his head dipped toward her, her knees locked and she pulled away. Hadn't she learned her lesson the first time? While she would definitely find pleasure in his arms, she wouldn't find the security she needed above all else. The situation was too uncertain, his attraction to her undoubtedly as fleeting as before.

He dropped his hands from her and looked away as if he had come to his senses, also. Who was she kidding? He probably couldn't believe she was practically throwing herself at him again.

With a cough he cleared his throat. "You okay? You didn't twist an ankle or anything?"

"No. I'm fine. Just peachy." She took a few more steps away and pushed her hair back from her face. She had to get a grip. Heading for her favorite rock, she took several deep breaths to slow her pulse.

"This sure is a great spot," he said from right behind her.

"Yeah, it is." She didn't look at him as she hoisted herself up to her seat and tried to pretend she didn't care when he propped his hip on her rock, his big, warm body inches from hers. But she did care. She cared so much she wanted to cry from the wanting, the needing.

Get over it, she scolded herself.

Harrison tried to focus on the dark-green water slipping by in front of him, but the woman seated next to him clamored for his attention on so many levels.

He didn't know what to think. One minute she looked at him as if he was the embodiment of the next great plague, then she beckoned him to get lost in the sun-warmed richness of her eyes. Maybe he was imagining things. His body sure was. Every inch of him was at attention, waiting for contact with her.

He drew in a deep breath of the fresh air and tried to stop thinking about making love with Juliet. The air down here reminded him of the earth after a drenching rain—clean, moist, lush. Like Juliet's mouth. He gave himself a shake and buried his hands in the pockets of his black pants.

"Cold?"

He latched on to the safe, uncomplicated subject. When in doubt talk about the weather. "No, not really. But it is quite a bit cooler down here than it is up at the store. It must be nice to be able to escape the late summer heat."

"I escape a lot of things down here." She brought her knees up to her chest.

Uh-oh. He knew that position. He didn't want to put her on the defensive, but he desperately wanted to get to know her. To understand. The most likely subject to give him an insight into her character was probably one of the least pleasant. He had to start somewhere, though.

"Your family drives you nuts, huh?"

She slanted him a wary look. "Doesn't yours?"

"Just my dad."

"Mmm."

Harrison readjusted his hip on the boulder, thinking he shouldn't have phrased his question about her family the way he had. "Have they always…" He struggled to describe her family without offending her.

"Just sat around?" she supplied neatly for him.

He shrugged apologetically.

"Believe it or not, no." She propped an elbow on her knee and rested her chin in her hand. "When Grandpa was alive, everyone had a job, of sorts. My brother worked up at the sawmill. He pulled logs on the green chain."

"That would explain his size."

"He lost that job over five years ago when they closed the mill."

"Oh."

She smiled. "He's all muscly now because he and his friends have a bunch of weights set up in the back of the garage they supposedly work at. Instead of fixing cars, they mostly just drink beer and pump iron."

Harrison thought it best not to comment.

She stared at the water for a moment before adding, "The closing of that mill affected a lot of folks in this area."

Even though none of Two Rivers's pulp suppliers were located on the McKenzie, he nonetheless felt the need to explain why such things happened. "They probably had to shut that one mill to keep from having to close all of them. I've had to do it myself to keep our company's bottom line healthy if a particular mill is too big a drain.''

"Well, it didn't do much for our bottom line." He didn't miss the censure in her tone. "Although Willie is supposed to start working at another mill sometime soon, I guess. That will help." She shrugged. "Mom used to do a halfway decent job with the store, but without Grandpa there to kick her in the rear now and then, she just sits at our kitchen table most of the time. Willie thinks she's counting the gold Formica speckles, but I think she's just sitting there.''

"Maybe she's still mourning your grandfather. That was her dad, right?''

Surprise crossed her face, then she nodded. "Yeah, he was." She gave him a speculative look.

"What about your father?''

She shrugged again. "Mom didn't know which of her boyfriends to point the finger at, so she left that particular line blank on my birth certificate. But it's okay. I had Grandpa.''

Harrison looked down at her, watching the breeze that rose off the water lift the sun-honeyed hair away from her beautiful face like an angel's sigh. Nothing she had told him about her family surprised him in the least. Their backgrounds fit with his perceptions of them. But nothing about Juliet fit. There was something about her that made her seem different from the other two. "And what about you, Juliet?''

"Me?''

"Yes, you.''

She lifted her chin from her hand and started to fidget, then wrapped her arms around her knees and pulled them tight to her chest as if to still herself. Or go into defense mode. "I'm just Nathan's mommy. Fortunately, I can be that and mind the store at the same time." A wry smile flitted across her full lips. "Though don't expect the canned beans to ever be on the shelves. I made the mistake of using them when I started teaching Nat how to count. Now he loves to stack them all over the place while he tries to count them."

A strange feeling filled Harrison's chest. "You're a good mother."

She gave a ghost of a shrug, but he noticed her gaze darted quickly over his face to gauge his sincerity. "I try."

"But what about your life...before?" He didn't know how else to ask the question without putting into words the guilt he could taste along with the moist air. When she glanced at him, he didn't look away.

"I was going to go to college. Eventually." Her eyes clouded over and she looked away. "Probably only community college, but still college."

"Really? Which one?" he asked, excited to learn she'd aspired to a higher education. That alone provided a partial explanation of why she seemed so different from her family. Ambition, other than the sort that came in the form of a paternity settlement, seemed to be in short supply in her mother and brother.

"Yes, really," she snapped. "Which one doesn't matter anymore, now does it?"

He pulled in his chin, a little surprised by her anger over the simple question. It seemed a strong reaction. "Why not?"

"Because," she answered sharply, and started to slide off the rock.

Harrison reached out and placed a stilling hand on her arm. "Juliet, please. Just talk to me."

"What good will it do?"

He released her arm. "It would let me get to know the mother of my child, the woman I...the woman who..." He floundered, afraid of saying too much. How could he explain how she affected him in a way he didn't understand? How he wanted her more than any woman he had ever known? He settled for something less intimate and revealing. "The woman who'll be raising him."

"Are you sure?" she challenged despite his earlier praise. "Are you sure it'll be me?"

"Not when you're belligerent like this I'm not," he shot back, then instantly regretted it.

She narrowed her eyes and thinned her lips. He slid his gaze to the swirling current of the river. It had a lot in common with his gut.

Harrison could feel her looking at him, but she didn't speak for several moments. Finally she said, "What, exactly, did you want to know about me?" She sounded as though she was agreeing to something distasteful but necessary.

Sighing, he set his hands on his hips. "I would like to know *you,* what you want out of life, what you dream about." He shrugged, feeling a little self-conscious. "What a person aspires to tells a lot about them."

She pulled in a noisy breath. "I'd always wanted to go away to school and study something that would pay enough money so I'd never have to come back here."

He looked at her, but she was staring at the river. "Money doesn't solve problems, Juliet. It only makes them different."

She scoffed. "Spoken like a true millionaire."

"Okay, if you want to go that way, let's say you were the millionaire. What would you be doing?"

"Certainly not standing here…"

He stared hard at her.

"I'd be on a tropical island somewhere. Just me and Nat."

"Really?" He found it telling that she included Nathan in her fantasy.

She shrugged.

Harrison sighed again. "What would you have studied in school?"

She glanced up at him. "If I didn't have to worry about money?"

"Yes. If you didn't have a care in the world."

She crossed her arms and leaned back against the rock, her expression wistful and heartbreakingly beautiful as she considered the river again. "I would have studied literature."

He kept the surprise out of his voice. "Literature?"

"Yeah."

"American or English?"

"Shakespeare."

"English." He smiled and studied her lovely face. What next?

She shrugged again. "Because of Grandpa. He loved Shakespeare. He had this old book with all of Shakespeare's works in it. He called it Bill's book." She laughed softly, sadly. "He used to recite poems and stuff up to me while I sat on the balcony and he pumped gas. That's why that stupid balcony is so special to me.''

A kindred sadness bloomed in Harrison's chest. ''You cared about your grandfather a lot, didn't you?''

She nodded. ''He's the one who named me Juliet.''

Harrison chuckled. ''And Willie...?''

''William,'' they both said together, meeting each other's smiling eyes.

Her transformation took his breath away. The haunted distrust was gone from her beautiful, gold-flecked brown eyes, and her smile made her face glow. The need to make this expression permanent was like a gauntlet he mentally lunged to pick up.

''My mom, she told you her name was Phyllis, right?''

Harrison scratched his head. ''You know, I'm not even sure I was formally introduced to her. Your brother just said she was your mother.''

''Yeah. Just my mom.'' She shook her head. ''Well, anyway. Do you want to know what her real name is?''

He raised his brows. ''Not Phyllis?''

She giggled. ''Ophelia.''

''Hamlet's crazy girlfriend.''

She laughed outright. ''Yeah. Does she have the 'do for it, or what?''

Harrison shook his head, wondering at it all. There was so much more to Juliet than the earthy sensuality he was having a hell of a time ignoring. ''So you'd study Shakespeare.''

''Yeah. I'd study Shakespeare.'' She shrugged again. ''Go figure.''

''Yeah,'' Harrison echoed her favorite word, his

gaze glued to a lock of her silky hair drifting across her lush lips. "Go figure."

He reached to brush the hair away, but found himself tracing the fullness of her lower lip with the pad of his thumb instead. God, she did things to him, made him feel things and want things he'd only felt and wanted with her.

He was somehow connected to Juliet. And despite knowing he shouldn't, he *wanted* Juliet the way he'd wanted the peace he'd found along this river that June day he and Juliet had discovered each other. Knowing it was the second stupidest thing he'd ever done in his life but not caring any more than he had two years ago, Harrison met Juliet's warm brown gaze and asked, "Can I kiss you?"

Chapter Six

Juliet stared into Harrison's smoldering eyes, certain her twisted, lonely heart was making her hear things. The last time he had asked her if he could kiss her they were in the shed laughing themselves to tears over Willie's attempt at a racing motorcycle, complete with fake flames made of tinfoil erupting from the back.

He had looked into her eyes and stepped into the emptiness of her heart. With nothing more than his yearning gaze he had filled her, completed her, made nothing else in the world matter but the intangible connection they shared.

She had been so surprised by a man asking and not just trying to take that she'd blurted, "You're asking?"

He'd blinked. "Is that so strange?"

She hadn't bothered with an explanation then but had kissed him instead.

And it was happening again.

She wasn't sure whether she leaned toward him or gave him some other sign, but the next thing she knew he'd captured her lips in a soul-shattering kiss. Once again he instantly melted the ice she'd encased herself in out of self-preservation. She was far from the ice princess with him. But could she ever be *his* princess?

Burrowing her fingers into his thick hair and tilting her head to allow him better access, she welcomed his hot, stroking tongue into her mouth and felt the fire clear to the soles of her bare feet. The boundaries between them, both physical and emotional, faded as he wrapped his strong, sheltering arms around her and pressed her against the large rock until she no longer knew or cared where she ended and he began.

He angled his mouth and deepened the kiss until she thought she'd die if he didn't devour her completely. But he was the one who moaned deep in his throat. Juliet soared with the same sense of power and purpose she had felt the first time she'd lit his fire. He slid one hand up her back and into her hair to cup her head, then brought the other over her ribs and up between them to cover her breast.

The heat of his hand seared her through the thin cotton of her shirt and his kneading and teasing of her peaked nipple made it her turn to moan. Juliet arched into him, wanting more, needing to match herself with him one more time. She kissed him with all the longing and passion trapped inside that she had thought would never get out.

As if he understood her need, without releasing her mouth from his tender onslaught, Harrison leaned his weight forward until she was bent back over the rock. He pulled his big hand from her breast and she whimpered her disappointment, but he trailed his hand down to the back of her thigh and raised her leg to his waist. He fit his body to hers through their clothes.

Light exploded behind her closed eyelids and she nearly came undone.

After hitching her knee at his waist, he released her leg and reached for her shirt, pulling it from her jeans and pushing it up above her breasts. He skimmed her belly with his palm before pushing his blunt fingers under her bra and finding the sensitive tip of one hard nipple.

Pulling his mouth from hers, he rasped, "God, Juliet, what you do to me."

She opened her eyes and met his hot, intense gaze, and inside her head the tiny voice she'd done a poor job of banishing whispered, *There* is *such a thing as soul mates.* And she wanted to answer the need blazing in his eyes more than she wanted to breathe.

She arched up again and recaptured his mouth, telling him with her kiss and her body what she could never tell him with words. *You're the only man I've ever wanted, Harrison Rivers.*

He answered her passion in kind, but she didn't dare consider what message he meant to send her. The hardness of his body said enough. He rocked against her and Juliet had to pull her mouth from his and gasp a lungful of cool air to keep from shattering right then and there. He used the opportunity to pull away enough to push her bra aside.

His breath was hot against her skin when he murmured, "You are so damn sexy," then captured between his lips the nipple he'd been teasing with his fingers.

No amount of cool air could keep Juliet from spiraling upward from the sensation of his warm, wet mouth on the peak of her breast. Only the weight of his body kept her down. Their bodies felt so perfectly matched, so perfectly meant for each other. There *had* to be such a thing as soul mates.

But then the other, nastier voice that had taken up permanent residence in her brain answered, *There is also such a thing as a guy who can't pass up a sure thing.*

The thought was like a bucket of cold river water being dumped on her. Untangling her fingers from his thick golden hair, Juliet slid her hands to his broad shoulders. It wasn't fair, this wanting. And giving herself to him again, especially like this, would not improve whatever opinion he might have of her. There was too much at stake here—her baby and her heart.

Ashamed of her weakness for him, she gently pushed at his shoulders. "Harrison, please. We have to stop."

He didn't resist or protest in any way. Juliet had never felt so respected in her entire life. Funny how she hated it.

Unwilling to discover what other emotions his eyes might hold, she kept her gaze on the river as she righted her clothes then separated from him by hoisting herself up on the rock and drawing her knees to her chest again.

He still didn't say a word.

Juliet sat in awkward silence for a long time as the enormity of what she'd done sank in. She hugged her arms around her tighter and closed her eyes to the river.

She needed to know if he realized it, too, though, so she dared a glance in his direction. The river's breeze ruffled his thick blond hair the same way his fingers did when he ran them through it in frustration.

His expression now was anything but frustrated. He looked blank. Utterly, completely blank.

Juliet filled her lungs with cool air and pulled her gaze from his handsome profile. Controlling his expressions must be some trick he used in the boardroom to mask his feelings and motivations. And heaven only knew what had motivated him to kiss her again. *Other than the fact you were so willing, of course,* the nasty voice interjected.

She'd kissed him again. Heck, she'd nearly made love to him on a rock. Her rock.

Telling him her secrets was bad enough. First she'd admitted Nathan was his child—something she'd sworn she wouldn't do—and then she told him the truth when he insisted on playing "What do you want to be when you grow up?"

She'd always kept her aspirations to herself out of self-defense. After all, Willie would bust a gut if he learned she dreamed of studying literature. But Harrison hadn't laughed. He'd even acted as if he thought it a reasonable dream for her to have had, that it was something she could have achieved if she'd had the chance. For some odd reason he seemed to believe in her when no one else ever did. Man, if that wasn't enough to make her fall for the guy...

She turned back to consider his profile again. Of course, studying Shakespeare was probably a common pursuit in Harrison's world. A world where no one worried about money.

A world she would never fit into.

Juliet ground her teeth at her own idiocy. What good was there in wanting something she could never have?

But Harrison got to her. He looked in her eyes like

a man writing songs. He drew her out no matter how deep she tried to bury her true self. She found herself letting him into the place she kept her deepest secrets. Heaven help her if it really was her soul. She should be keeping her soul safe from Harrison, because her heart was already his.

"We need to get back," she said, stepping from the river's edge without sparing him a glance, still afraid of what he might see in her eyes.

"There's something we need to talk about first," he insisted.

Her gaze on the river, Juliet stopped even though her mind screamed for her to run.

"Juliet, I..."

With her heart hammering in her chest as she stared at the river, she waited for him to finish, to either give her hope or damn her to an existence she already knew. As the seconds ticked by and he didn't finish, her pulse slowed to a dull thud. How could she have forgotten this was the man who believed it was never a good thing to love someone so much he lost control?

In a flat tone she said it for him. "Let's pretend this," she gestured toward the rock, still not looking at him, "never happened."

"No, that's not what I was going—"

"That's the way I want it." She almost laughed. She wanted so many things that could never be. Furious at herself for wanting him, she repeated, "We should get back." She headed for the trail and trudged up it, digging her bare toes into the loose dirt and gravel. She could hear Harrison following in her wake.

She crested the incline and halted at the edge of

the road, but not because of the traffic occasionally speeding by. She was brought up short by the sight of a white van, the words Toys-N-Stuff emblazoned on its side in bright colors, parked behind Harrison's car. Dorothy Rivers flitted about the van's open rear doors.

Juliet watched, her mouth gaping, as Harrison's grandmother gaily directed the unloading of box after box of toys and child-size furniture. And Willie was right there next to the petite woman, jumping up and down and crowing his approval like an eight-year-old.

The takeover had begun. First Harrison stole her heart, now the Riverses were buying Nathan.

Her vision clouded, and she burst into a run toward the van, mindless of anything save stopping the bribing of her child.

She was vaguely aware of Harrison's shout of "Wait", of his hand clutching unsuccessfully at the back of her T-shirt, but she didn't break her stride as she darted across the road.

She heard Willie yell, "Hey, Grandma Rivers," distracting Dorothy from directing the van's driver where to put the toys. "You know, Nat would learn a lot more from Sesame Street if he watched it on a big-screen TV." Spotting Juliet charging toward him, Willie hailed her. "Jules! Look!" He pointed at the interior of the delivery van. "Christmas in July!"

"It's September," Ashley corrected mildly as she watched the unloading of the van.

"Who gives a rip? This is way cool," Willie said to Juliet when she came to a stop at his side, staring at him in horror. Taking a radio-controlled car from one of the deliverymen, he whistled through his teeth. "I've always wanted one of these."

Harrison's grandmother stepped away and put a hand on Willie's arm. "I'm sure Nathan will gladly share all *his* new toys with you."

Juliet panted, "No. No, he won't!" Strangled emotions, not exertion, made talking difficult.

Dorothy furrowed her delicate brow. "Oh, but he seems to know how to share just fi-"

Juliet cut her off. "I'm sorry, but they're all going back."

Dorothy pulled her chin in. "For heaven's sake, why?"

"Aww, Jules," Willie whined, and turned his face to the sky.

She heard the crunch of Harrison's footsteps on the gravel as he approached them, but Juliet didn't turn to look at him. She was too mad.

"Nothing is going back." Harrison said from behind her. "Well, at least not *all* of it. Good gracious, Grandmother, is there anything left in the store?"

Dorothy brought her narrow shoulders up and looked as though she was trying to appear contrite, but couldn't quite manage it. "I suppose I did get a tad carried away. But you did say I could buy him a little something."

"Grandmother, a jam-packed delivery van is *not* a little something."

The firmness of Harrison's tone surprised Juliet. She glanced at him. With his fists propped on his lean hips, his expression matched his tone, and only his slightly mussed hair hinted at the passion that had erupted between them. He continued to glare at the small woman until Juliet noticed a sparkle enter his eyes exactly like the one lighting his grandmother's gaze.

How would she ever make them understand if they all thought this a grand joke?

Harrison looked to her and the glint of amusement faded from his expression. "You have every right to return all but the most appropriate of the gifts."

"All but—" she scanned what was left in the van and reached for a plump, fuzzy brown bear, since Nat loved bears "—this...is going back. We don't need your charity," she said firmly. If she allowed anything but the smallest of gifts now, it wouldn't be long before Willie got his big-screen TV.

Harrison frowned. "Juliet—"

"I mean it."

His grandma stepped forward and lightly touched Juliet's hand. "Juliet, dear, he *is* my first and only great-grandchild," she pleaded in the softest of voices.

Juliet's mouth opened and closed, but she couldn't make the refusal come out. This tiny, elegant lady wasn't the scary, rich broad Juliet needed her to be, and she found it difficult to hold on to her resolve.

Harrison came to Juliet's rescue, taking both her and his grandmother by the arm and leading them toward Nathan playing with a new shovel and bucket under the willow tree. The heat of his palm against her flesh made it hard for her to think. "How about if we put a firm limit on the gifts, right here, right now."

"Perhaps I should only bring him a sweet," Dorothy mused, considering the filthy toddler. "You did say he was partial to licorice, didn't you, Harrison?"

Harrison smiled down at his son when the mention of his favorite candy brought the child's attention to them. "Let's stick with more nutritious treats from now on."

"No strawberries," Juliet interjected. "They make him swell up."

Dorothy sighed and got a dreamy, wistful look on her face. "Just like his daddy."

Juliet silently groaned. "I don't want him—" she started to flounder at the understanding she saw in Harrison's eyes.

"Spoiled," he supplied for her. "Neither do I. I don't want him excited to see us only because we bring him presents. I want him to love us for us."

Juliet's breath caught in her throat, and a dull, thick sensation settled in her belly. Great. Instead of buying her child's love, the Riverses intended to earn it.

AS HE DROVE AWAY from the little store, one thought tormented Harrison. He wanted to make love to Juliet again.

He couldn't think about it. If he did, who knew what conclusions he might come to, what crazy, irrational notions he might consider possible. But with every curve of the road came memories of Juliet against him, the feel of her heat surrounding him.

She affected him as much as, no, more than the first time he'd held her in his arms. She was no longer a young woman experimenting with passion, she was a grown woman who knew exactly what that passion could cost her but had wanted to pay the price all the same. Until she'd come to her senses.

Thank God one of them had.

Today he had proved himself irresponsible beyond measure for the second time in his life. The last thing he should be doing was reliving the moment. Besides, he had his grandmother sitting beside him.

Her silence was telling.

Harrison shifted in the seat of his car and forced his fingers to relax their grip on the steering wheel. The road back down the river wasn't that difficult to negotiate. But Grandmother must have formed some serious opinions, for her to keep them to herself like this.

While Dorothy Rivers might not possess as much calm wisdom as her husband had, she made up for it with a spunky cleverness. Or maybe it was feminine intuition, because his mother had had it, too. Whatever the case, Grandmother keeping her opinions to herself was annoying as hell and left him with no alternative but to think about his disastrous weakness for Juliet. Ashley was no help, either, having long ago run out of synonyms for *interesting*.

She found his *situation* with Juliet and Nathan *interesting*. Especially the fact that he hadn't returned to see Juliet sooner—Juliet being, in her estimation, a lovely girl. Lord save him from his sister's meddling streak.

"Well?" he demanded, unable to take his grandmother's silence anymore.

"Well, what, dear?" she answered obtusely.

"What do you think?"

"I think we had a very interesting afternoon."

Ashley practically snickered in the back seat and he glanced at his grandmother, his heart thundering at the thought that they knew what he and Juliet had been doing down by the river. "Interesting?"

"Most decidedly." She nodded and refolded her slight hands in her lap.

Harrison only then noticed how dirty she was and snorted, realizing she meant her time with Nathan. "Interesting, my butt. You had a ball."

She smiled in response. Then she said, "Nathan is absolutely, utterly adorable, Harrison. Whatever happens, I will not allow you to lose contact with that cherub."

"I agree with you completely, Grandmother. That's the only thing I've been certain of from the beginning." He let out a heavy breath, his inability to control himself around Juliet getting to him. He could not allow himself to become physically involved with her again. Her soft, brown eyes, beguiling smile and understanding touch reached places inside of him he'd thought securely shored up.

For the first time in his life, he feared his heart might be in jeopardy from a woman. And if he was to avoid his father's fate, he couldn't open himself up to that kind of vulnerability.

"We'll have to take steps to ensure Nathan remains a part of our family," she said with her trademark finality.

Harrison's brows shot up. "Such as?"

"Marriage is the obvious answer."

He nearly choked on his tongue and Ashley breathed, "Oh, my."

Dorothy waved a dismissive hand in the air. "All right. Let me think on it."

"Grandmother," Harrison warned, disliking her train of thought. He was entirely open to any and all ideas, barring marriage. His inability to keep his distance from Juliet placed serious doubt on the wisdom of bringing Juliet and Nathan home with him as it was.

The more he thought on it, the more relieved he became that she hadn't allowed him to broach the subject down by the river after they'd kissed. Kissed, hell, they'd damn near erupted in flames. Having her underfoot would not allow him to regain his focus on work. Or keep his heart locked up tight, safe from her sunflower-center eyes and soothing touches.

"Now, Juliet. She's…intriguing," Grandmother offered.

Harrison snorted again at her variation on Ashley's understatement.

His grandmother arched an eyebrow at him. "Are you catching a cold, dear?"

"No, Grandmother."

"Then do stop snorting at me. You sound disturbingly like your father."

"Good Lord," he said, appalled.

"Exactly."

"But to describe Juliet as intriguing, well…" He laughed and shook his head. It was like calling the ceilings of the Sistine Chapel merely *colorful*.

His grandmother shifted in her seat and faced him. "You find her intriguing, though, don't you?"

He felt himself flush. "*Intriguing* isn't quite the word I'd use." More like irresistible. Compelling. Entirely unsuitable for an aspiring Chairman of the Board. But what she had confided in him down by the river thrust itself to the forefront of his mind. "She told me today that had she been able to go to college as she'd planned—"

Both of Grandmother's delicate brows went up and she smiled broadly. "She'd planned on attending college? What kept her—"

Ashley discreetly coughed in the back seat.

His grandmother colored. "Never mind."

Harrison returned his attention to the road, but an image of Juliet's wistful expression as she talked about her dreams nagged at him. "She would have studied literature. Shakespeare to be exact."

"Interesting," Ashley murmured and earned a look over his shoulder.

"Imagine." Grandmother's tone was one of wonder.

"Yes. Imagine."

Juliet would have undoubtedly made the most of the bohemian lifestyle literature majors seemed to favor, sitting in coffee shops discussing the genius of the Bard until the wee hours.

He gave himself a slight shake. The fact remained that hadn't happened. "But only if she hadn't had any money worries. Obviously, that wasn't the case."

"Obviously."

From the corner of his eye he could see his grandmother tapping a finger on her chin. "You've learned some interesting things about the mother of your child today."

Harrison started to snort again, but stopped himself in time.

"What do you intend to do with this new information?"

He glanced at her. What, indeed? Then an idea occurred to him. He turned his gaze back to the road. "While I can't turn back the clock, I can remove one obstacle Juliet had in the pursuit of her dreams."

"Which is?" Her voice revealed the excitement she always confessed to experiencing when she discovered a new cause to champion.

"Money. Juliet would have pursued a degree in

literature if money weren't an issue. I can make that happen for her.''

Ashley said, "She seems determined not to take anything from you. I seriously doubt she will accept any sort of financial aid you might extend to her.''

"That's where Grandmother can help me.'' He inclined his head toward her. "You're a pro at helping people without making them feel like charity cases.''

His grandmother nodded in understanding. "And I am certain that is the one thing Juliet does not wish to be perceived as.''

Though Juliet might not wish to be perceived that way, perhaps thinking of her in such terms would help him get a grip on his attraction to her. After all, one didn't generally lust after one's favorite charity.

JULIET GRUNTED and hoisted the last load of yellowed newspaper into the bed of Willie's truck. Putting her hands to the small of her aching back, she tilted her chin and let the sun dry the perspiration from her face. Man, it was hot. Of course, lugging six months worth of newspapers out to the truck tended to heat a body up.

Almost as much as being in Harrison Rivers's arms. Her body tightened in response.

She moaned and dropped her chin, surveying the piles of papers and junk she'd stacked in the back of the truck as she willed her focus back to what she was doing. She had done more cleaning in the past day and a half than she'd done in the past six months. But Juliet couldn't shake the image of Dorothy Rivers pretending not to see what a dump the place was.

And then there was Harrison. He hadn't said a word, but Juliet knew he was concerned about his son living in such a mess. And he'd probably judged her to be a loser for allowing her home to get that way.

Well, no more. She'd bust her hump if she had to, to clean the place up and get it looking halfway decent. She eyed the strips of dark, just-turned soil forming a path of sorts to the door and beneath the edge of her balcony. Flower beds filled with mums should make a huge difference.

She moved away from the truck, intent on yanking Willie from the couch to send him to the recycling center and landfill. Nathan could help her dust the store. He didn't need to veg-out on the floor watching the tube all day like his uncle. But the sound of tires on gravel stopped her.

Squinting against the flash of sun glinting off a windshield, Juliet watched a well-polished, black Mercedes pull into the parking lot.

Harrison.

Her heart leaped. It didn't plummet, grind to a stop or drop to the soles of her feet. It leaped.

Great.

Determined to still the wild fluttering inside her, Juliet set her mouth in a grim line.

The car stopped in front of her, and the driver's door swung open. She had to bring her back teeth together against the surge of excitement she felt at the sight of Harrison. He was so handsome in his khaki pants and lightweight denim shirt, its sleeves rolled up to reveal his tanned, muscular forearms.

"Morning, Juliet," Harrison called, shutting his door.

"Hey." She dropped her shielding hand and used the sun as an excuse to squint and hide any need that might show in her eyes.

Looking past her, Harrison called, "There's Daddy's boy!"

Juliet turned in time to see Nat jerk to a stop halfway between them and the door to the store. He stood very still, his shoulders rounded, a delighted look on his little face.

Harrison moved to stand next to Juliet, his elbow brushing hers, and she glanced up at him, prepared to tell him what Nathan was doing. Most people couldn't figure the game out.

The explanation died in her throat.

His smile deeply grooved his cheek and crinkles rayed out from the corner of his eye. He chuckled and she felt it in her chest, then he looked down at her. It was there in the warmth of his river-green eyes.

He knew.

Swallowing past the lump in her throat, Juliet said, "My mom thinks we should tell him he isn't really hiding."

"I wouldn't dream of it," Harrison pledged. He winked at her and started off toward Nat, his gaze on everything but the giggling toddler. "Where's Nathan?" he wondered loudly. Harrison didn't get closer than two feet before the little boy couldn't bear it any longer and launched himself at his father's legs.

"Here!" Nathan squealed.

Harrison clutched at his heart. "Oh! You surprised me!" He bent and hugged Nathan against his legs.

"Hide, Dada. Hide." Nathan jumped up and down within his father's gentle embrace, tugging on his father's pants.

"Okay, okay," Harrison laughed. Peeling away Nathan's hands, he guided the toddler's fat palms up to cover his eyes. "But no peeking."

Harrison hurried toward Juliet and grabbed her hand, threading his warm fingers through hers. It seemed to have become a habit with him. "You too, Mommy," he said in a deep, husky voice and pulled her along with him to hide behind the willow tree, their son watching them through his splayed fingers the entire way.

With the rough bark of the tree against her back and Harrison's big, spicy-smelling body pressed to her side, Juliet closed her eyes against the bittersweet emotions ricocheting through her. He was so good with Nathan. The way a father should be. She fleetingly wondered if her own father, whichever one of her mom's boyfriends he'd been, would have been as good with her, if he'd had the chance.

She was right not to deny Harrison that chance. No matter how much having him in their lives cost her.

As he watched Nathan imitate his father's earlier feigned search, Harrison leaned his head down and whispered in her ear, "This is so much fun. I haven't felt this happy in a very long time."

The heat of his breath sent a delicious shiver clear to her toes. By the time she rode it out and leaned away so she could turn and look at him, he'd returned his attention to Nathan romping about in joyful hysterics.

Juliet stared at Harrison's perfect profile. Was he implying that he wasn't happy in Richville? Juliet quirked her mouth. Aside from missing his mother, she hadn't considered that Harrison's life might be lacking. For what? The love of a good woman?

She looked away and fisted her free hand—the other still held prisoner by Harrison's big paw—against the sudden, ridiculous hope surging through her heart. The only thing Harrison's life lacked was an adorable little boy to play with all the time. Considering how easily he'd swept her off her feet, he probably had *suitable* women crawling out of the mahogany woodwork. She shouldn't, *wouldn't,* care what he needed.

She felt him lean toward her again, whether to whisper something else in ear or what, she didn't want to know, but Nathan chose that moment to lunge at their legs. Harrison bent to grab him. The ringing of a cell phone fastened to his belt stopped him. He directed Nathan toward Juliet and stepped away to answer the call.

"What is it?" he clipped out. Apparently the boss didn't have to bother with hello.

Juliet snagged Nathan when he started to charge his father, but she didn't step away. She was unable to resist listening in on what the corporate-bigwig side of Harrison sounded like. She watched in fascination as he spread his feet wide, planted his hand on his hip and frowned fiercely, clearly not pleased with what was being said to him.

"No. Look, I covered all of that during the last board meeting. If they missed the pertinent facts, they can go over the figures themselves." He listened for a minute, then said, "No. No, I won't. They'll just have to trust me on that. And remind them whose name is on the company while you're at it." He pushed the end button and clipped the phone back on his belt. Without so much as taking a calming breath, he turned and spread his hands in welcome to his son. His expression had changed from formidable to fatherly in the blink of an eye.

As she released her son to run to his father's arms,

reality hit Juliet once again like a ton of bricks. She focused on the man scooping her precious baby up into his arms with laughter and noisy kisses.

Was the man that held her and Nathan in his arms and made them feel so safe the real Harrison Rivers? Or was he the man who shut down mills, put the almighty bottom line above all else and believed it was never good to love someone too much?

"I wouldn't know," Juliet whispered past a suddenly tight throat.

Because she didn't know Harrison Rivers at all.

HARRISON HALTED in the process of tossing Nathan up in the air again, his attention snagging on the woman watching him. She looked like summer and sunshine in her simple white T-shirt and denim cutoffs. Feeling her pull on him, he set Nathan on his forearm and strode toward her.

He took a deep breath as he came to stand before her. He had to get control of himself. He couldn't allow himself to give in to this weakness for Juliet that threatened to lure him over the line he'd drawn between them. He couldn't give in to his passion again. His vow to hold his heart safe was being tested as it was. He'd already succumbed to Nathan. Lord only knew the sort of pain he'd be opening himself up to if he succumbed to Juliet. Loving Mom so much had nearly cost Dad everything.

He tried to ask a casual question, but he couldn't help the suggestiveness of his tone. "What would you like to do now?"

"You must be hot. I'll get you two boys something to drink," Juliet said in a rush and started for the door.

Wanting nothing more than her presence, Harrison tried to stop her. "Juliet—"

"Juice, Momma," Nathan interrupted him. "Juice!"

She didn't acknowledge either of them before she disappeared inside.

Harrison resumed making his son squeal in delight by lifting him above his head until Juliet emerged from the store with two glass mugs of lemonade in one hand and a cup with a lid in the other.

"Down," Nathan demanded, so Harrison set him on the ground.

Juliet bent to hand Nathan his drink saying, "This is for you." She straightened and to Harrison said, "And this is for you." She offered him the glass, but her gaze had gone back to where their son sat on the ground, draining his cup with big gulps.

"Thank you." He took the mug, capturing her fingers beneath his in the process. She glanced up at him, her gaze searching his, before she pulled her hand away. She must think he was a real piece of work.

Then he remembered the olive branch he'd brought with him. "Hey, I have something for you, too." He went to his car and set his glass on the hood so he could retrieve the manila envelope from his briefcase in the back seat.

She wandered after him. "Your Porsche in the shop?"

"Nope. Traded it for this one. It wasn't exactly a family car." Envelope in hand, he grinned in anticipation as he turned and handed it to her. "Here you go."

"What's this?" Her suspicion was clear in her tone and the narrowing of her glorious brown eyes.

"Just look," he urged. Harrison wasn't certain, but he thought her hands shook when she broke the envelope's seal. Had no one ever given her a surprise before? No one besides him, that is. Thank goodness this was one she would be pleased to receive. His grin widened in anticipation. There was definitely something to be said for this Prince Charming, Fairy Godfather, whatever routine.

After removing the papers inside, she began to read them. She flipped through the pages twice before raising her eyes to his.

Harrison nearly took a step back from the force of the recrimination in her expression.

Her lip curled and her eyes narrowed. She grated out, "How dare you."

Chapter Seven

Harrison blinked. Of all the reactions he'd imagined receiving from her, anger hadn't been one of them. "Beg your pardon?"

Juliet pulled in a shaky breath, her fingers crushing the papers in her hand. "I said, how dare you. How dare you mess with my life like this."

"I'm not messing—"

"Yes you are! And that's all you've done since the first second I saw you."

He stared at her in confusion. "But you said, down by the river, that you'd planned on going to college before—"

"Before you messed with my—"

"I'm sorry I didn't come back, Juliet," he cut her off, losing the battle with his disappointment and frustration. He'd wanted so much to do something for her, to somehow make amends. "I'm sorry."

"I'm sure you're sorry you ever set eyes, or anything else, on me," she said in a hard tone, and Harrison wasn't sure if it was directed at him or herself.

"No." Stepping closer, he took hold of her upper arm. "I will never, ever regret finding you." His voice dropped a notch. "I can't even make myself regret what happened between us." Harrison closed his eyes in remembrance and filled his lungs with summer-tinged air to steady himself against the heady images in his head.

She'd felt so wonderful in his arms. So right.

Opening his eyes, he glanced over at his son trying to hold an ant. "And I sure as hell don't regret creating that little bit of magic over there. What I *do* regret is how..." He looked back down at her and had to swallow when he saw the moisture glistening in her big, brown eyes. "How I handled things after the first time."

"You didn't *handle things*." She dropped her gaze from his, focusing instead on the front of his shirt. "You kissed me goodbye and left."

She was right. He'd said goodbye and driven back to his life, back to his reality, thinking he was free to focus on achieving the one and only goal he'd ever had in life—running his grandfather's company. "That's right," he whispered past the thickness in his throat. "And I held the memory of you, of us, close, like I would any fantasy come true. It wasn't long before I halfway doubted that it *had* really happened."

She looked over at their son. "Oh, it happened, all right."

"I know that. But I guess pretending it hadn't was how I dealt with what I'd done, the impulses I'd given in to. The pain I'd needed help getting past." He gently squeezed her arm, hoping she'd recognize his earnestness. "And that's why I'm trying to make it right. I never meant to rob you of what you'd planned for your life, Juliet." He nodded at the papers she held tightly in her hands. "That's why I enrolled you at the community college in Eugene—"

"So that's how you're going to pay me off? Foot the bill for me to go to school and study..." She flipped through the papers again until she reached the schedule of classes he'd signed her up for. "English Lit 101?" She met his gaze again, a light-brown eyebrow raised.

"I'm not paying you off." He dropped his hand from her arm, feeling like the thief he was. He had stolen so much from her with his recklessness, yet he still found himself wanting more. "I'm not paying for anything. You've been awarded a full-ride scholarship." He shifted on his feet, conscious of not being entirely truthful.

"How? For what? I seriously doubt Lane Community College has a river-watching team."

"For being a single mother. There's a scholarship fund set up for single mothers. So they can go to school and make something of their lives."

She flipped through the papers again. "It says here this 'scholarship' is given by the Rivers Foundation. My, what a coincidence."

"It's legitimate, Juliet."

"Oh, really. And how long, exactly, has it been around?"

He planted his hands on his hips and seriously considered lying to her, but knew there was no point. She could discover the truth easily enough. "Not long. And I admit your situation gave me the idea."

"Oh, so I'm a *situation* now. Well, I don't want it." She slapped the papers against his chest and turned to walk away.

Harrison fumbled to catch them. "For God's sake, why?"

"Because I don't need pity or to have my life manipulated—"

"I'm not manipulating you!" Clutching the papers to his chest, he followed after her. If only he had a free hand to shake some sense into her. Didn't she understand this was the least he could do for so drastically changing her life? "If you don't want to take the courses I signed you up for, you don't have to—"

"I don't want you controlling me."

He sighed and prayed for patience. "I won't be controlling you. I won't have anything to do with your schooling."

"Oh, and like the Rivers Foundation's Scholarship for Unwed Mothers, or whatever you've named it, won't be notified when I flunk a class."

He brought his brows down. "What makes you think you'll fail a class?"

She crossed her arms over her chest, her shoulders hunched up high.

A light bulb came on in his head. "You don't want to go to school because you're afraid of failing."

"My, don't you belong on Oprah," she gibed, but wouldn't meet his gaze. "What I'm afraid of is you taking our son from me."

He forced himself to focus on getting her acquiescence, not on her admission and those two wonderful words *our son.* "It's okay to fail, Juliet. You learn from it and try again."

"You can afford to fail." She scoffed. "Some of us aren't so lucky."

"But you have to at least try. How will you ever

know what you can achieve if you won't take the risk?''

She finally looked up at him. ''The last time—that is, the only time—I took a risk...'' She paused, her lip quivering and her eyes bright with unshed tears. Bitterness spilled over into her voice. ''I got nailed— literally. So forgive me if I'm not in any all-fire hurry to go for something again. Why can't things stay the way they are? Nobody's going to get hurt if you'd leave things the way they are.'' She went to Nathan and picked him up before retreating into the store, the screen door slamming in her wake.

Harrison looked down at the crumpled papers he still held trapped against his chest. So, she thought it was easier—and safer—to leave things as they were. She was afraid to take the chance that life might hold possibilities for her. Possibilities that would take her out of her comfort zone, out of the world she knew.

He raised his gaze to the tilting balcony with its lone chair. She'd been sitting there the first time he'd seen her, and he remembered wondering what could a gorgeous woman like her be waiting for up there? And she was still waiting. For the courage to take another risk? Or for someone to push her into taking one?

After retrieving the lemonade glasses, he went into the store, not surprised to find it empty, and placed the drinks and the envelope on the checkout counter. Juliet would realize her dreams, even if he had to haul her along by the scruff of her beautiful neck to do it.

JULIET DRAGGED her bare heels back and forth over the balcony rail, inadvertently cleaning off the final layer of peeling white paint. It was all too much. The river of change swamping her life had picked up so much speed she was finally drowning in the murky current.

Harrison expected her to go to college. She couldn't. While she was a heck of a lot smarter than the rest of her family, taking after Grandpa and all, she wasn't smart enough for college. Or was she?

Harrison might as well have asked her to walk on the moon. Something to dream about but never do. No one in her world had ever gone to college. No one could tell her what to expect and reassure her.

No one but Harrison.

Juliet didn't want him to know how much the unknown scared her spitless. She tilted her chair on its back legs and stared up at the late-afternoon sky, its color faded by the heat. If only Grandpa were still here to help her figure out what to do. He would be able to help her see the right way of things. And she sure needed some guidance now. She so desperately wanted to do right by Nat. If only she knew what right was.

She closed her eyes and dropped her head onto the back of her chair, only vaguely aware of the phone ringing downstairs. Probably Harrison calling to bug her some more. As if he hadn't already done enough.

"Jules, it's for you!" Willie shouted up the stairs at her.

Juliet groaned and let her chair back down on all four legs with a soft *thunk*. She better not be right. And Willie better not have woken Nat with his bellowing. He knew Nat was napping.

After a quick look-see into Nathan's crib, she was reassured he had, indeed, worn himself out too much this morning playing with his father to be disturbed by his loudmouthed uncle. Closing the door quietly behind her, she hurried downstairs.

With Willie nowhere in sight, she gave the phone the walleye for a second as it swung by its cord before she mustered the courage to pick it up, put it to her ear and acknowledge whoever waited on the other end.

Halfway hoping, halfway dreading to hear Harrison's voice, she said, "Hello?"

A woman's voice answered her. "Juliet? This is Dorothy Rivers."

Juliet heaved a sigh of relief. Sort of.

After the usual pleasantries—usual in Dorothy's world, that is—Nathan's great-grandmother's tone changed subtly and Juliet knew Dorothy was about to get down to business.

"I know this is extremely short notice and rather abrupt, dear," Dorothy said. "But I desperately need your help."

HER HANDS STICKY with perspiration, Juliet readjusted her grip on the wheel of Willie's truck and wished for the millionth time she'd had the guts to tell Dorothy Rivers no. 'Course it hadn't been until Juliet had hung up the phone and climbed halfway up the stairs that it dawned on her what Dorothy had talked her into doing.

Just because she was an unwed mother didn't mean she was an expert on them. And how in the world was she supposed to go up to these girls and convince them to try to get a scholarship she herself didn't want? But Dorothy had convinced her that she could approach poor, unwed mothers in a way a rich patron couldn't.

The rich patron hadn't knocked up these other girls, though. Harrison must have told his grandmother how badly he'd blown it when he'd tried to give her the scholarship.

The old gal had fought dirty—she'd brought Nathan, and all the other innocent babes, into the discussion. Juliet wanted her baby to grow up proud of his mother, and she was sure these other young women felt the same way. So Dorothy had convinced her to help. Too bad she and Nathan had to go to the Rivers estate to do it.

Oh, man.

Juliet glanced down at her floral rayon dress and prayed she looked okay. She had to, because this dress was all she owned that wasn't denim and frayed. Not exactly what one would wear to a millionaire's house.

Oh, man.

For courage she looked at the beautiful baby next to her, happily shredding the directions to the estate. Thank heaven he'd stayed clean. His overalls with the little trains were getting short, but they were still cute on him. Even with bits of paper sprinkled all over them.

"Nathan, let Mommy have that please," she said, and reached to take the torn paper from his hand.

Rechecking what was left of the instructions, she slowed Willie's truck so she wouldn't miss the turn to the Riverses' private drive.

She shouldn't have worried. The huge, black-iron gate with the Rivers name fashioned out of metal was hard to miss. The gate reminded her of the entrance to an old graveyard. But instead of being all rusted and broken-down, the fancy scrolled-iron gate gleamed in the noontime sun and swung silently open as she approached, closing with finality once she was through. She checked for some sort of security booth hidden in the perfect shrub wall on either side of the gate but didn't see one. Probably operated remotely by satellite, she thought sarcastically.

Juliet cussed silently as she drove up the gently curving, dark-gray cobblestone drive. One more example of how different she and Harrison were. She'd grown up in a dump while he'd grown up in a park. That was the only way she could think to describe the perfect lawn, flowers and trees casually but definitely arranged on either side of the drive.

The green of the grass and the reds and yellows and purples of the different kinds of flowers were so vibrant she mumbled, "We're not in Kansas anymore, Toto."

The farther up the drive they went, the more formal the planting arrangements became. A low boxwood hedge curved in toward the drive to frame it, and Juliet wondered if Harrison planned to eventually marry some debutante in the midst of the rose garden on the right. Some debutante he wouldn't love too much, of course. The thought made her chest hurt.

Too easily she remembered him saying he *needed* her, and the words he'd whispered in her ear after he'd made that first tentative touch in the back shed. He'd said he felt that they'd been *predestined* to be together.

That one word had helped her through the worst parts of her pregnancy, had helped her believe their child hadn't simply been a mistake. Now did he believe that he was *predestined* to marry one of his own kind in a rose garden?

"Like it matters to you," Juliet stubbornly told herself and focused her attention back on the cobblestones.

Then the house came into view. Juliet's jaw dropped.

It was big, brick and had lots of windows. Make that huge, with a ton of windows, the tops of some stained glass. The house was beautiful. Church beautiful. She felt as if she had warped into the English countryside and was driving up to some duke's estate. She had only seen houses like this on those old-fashioned, British detective shows she loved to watch on public television.

No wonder Harrison had wanted to bring Nathan here to play. How long before he would want Nathan to live here?

And how could she say no?

Hating the crushing weight she felt every time she thought of losing her child, she maneuvered the truck past the half-dozen luxury cars parked along the circular drive in front of the house.

"The Riverses have way too many cars, Nathan baby."

"Outside!" He pointed to the vast, velvety-looking lawn. "Outside!"

"Maybe later, baby," she said as she parked the truck.

She lifted Nathan out and carried him up the wide stone steps leading to the beautifully carved double doors of the mansion. Shifting him to her hip, she raised a fist, uncertainly eyeing the doors' iron lion's head knockers, but the right door opened before she could lay a knuckle to the wood.

On the other side a slender man in a simple black

suit smiled and inclined his head as he moved back out of the way. "Miss Jones and Master Nathan! Mrs. Rivers has been expecting you."

A butler, no less. Juliet swallowed heavily and stepped inside. Then froze in her tracks. She shouldn't have been surprised. Really, she shouldn't have. But the sight of the large black-and-white marble-tiled foyer with its huge, curving staircase, a large round table sporting an oriental-looking vase full of fresh flowers bigger than her head, topped off with a crystal chandelier the size of a Volkswagen Bug stunned her. It was like walking into the classiest of hotels. Only this wasn't a hotel. This was Harrison's home. She was *so* out of her element.

The butler closed the door behind her. The latch clicking home startled her back to life. He reached for the diaper bag slung over her shoulder and politely asked, "May I?"

"Sure. But don't stash it too far away. He hasn't done his big job yet." She patted Nathan's bottom, then mentally cringed. While he didn't show any outward reaction, now the butler knew she had no class. *Great start, Jules.*

"Oh, and here." She handed him Willie's keys, noticing too late the miniature beer can key chain. "Just shove 'em…" She waved at the diaper bag. The beer can went just great with the teddy bear design on the bag. She turned and headed down the wood-paneled entryway, furious at her nervousness.

The butler hurried to catch up with her and proceeded to lead her through the house.

And what a house.

She caught glimpses of some of the rooms that opened directly off the large, rectangle foyer. There was an office with a huge desk, a dining room with a huge table, a library with wall-to-wall books and a not-so-huge piano. It was all so...so...decorated. But not in a gaudy or overdone way, despite the size of some of the pieces. The house and its furnishings gave off the same kind of vibes as Dorothy Rivers— and Harrison and Ashley, for that matter. Those vibes said *money,* but didn't scream it at you. In a word, the Rivers family had *class.*

Juliet's focus shifted to keeping Nathan's curious little paws off the vases and other pricey-looking knickknacks—namely pointless looking glass and marble balls—hanging out on a constant string of skinny tables placed below large paintings. The artwork, for the most part, matched the formal style of the house, with horses and countrysides—except for a few modernish, splashes-of-color-type paintings that were as surprising as Dorothy herself.

Juliet didn't realize the butler had led her straight through the house until they stepped out onto the back veranda. She found herself face-to-beet-red-face with a group of women. And not one of them looked remotely like an underprivileged, unwed mother. Or under the age of fifty.

The gathering looked more like a garden party, complete with white-linen-covered tables and matching folding chairs scattered around.

She'd been had.

"Juliet, darling!" Dorothy separated herself from the knot of women and hurried to Juliet's side with what seemed to be genuine pleasure. "I'm so glad you could come. I was just telling my friends what a lovely young woman you are and how utterly adorable my great-grandbaby is." She put a loving hand on Nathan's back and pressed a kiss to his willing cheek.

In a low, accusing tone Juliet said, "You said you needed me to talk to other women *like me* about the scholarship."

Dorothy stepped to Juliet's other side and leaned in close. "I do, I do. But first I need your help in convincing these dear ladies to *fund* the scholarship. Society matrons can be surprisingly tightfisted at times, I'm afraid."

Mortified, Juliet croaked, "I'm not some poster child, Dorothy. And I'm sure not going to let you use Nathan—"

"Pish." Dorothy cut her off, then looped an arm through Juliet's. "I've thought no such thing. And I swear on my sweet husband's soul I would never use this angel in any way, shape or form. Nor have I gone into any great detail regarding your, er, relationship with Harrison."

Dorothy patted Juliet's arm. "The fact is, you are clearly an intelligent young woman who can speak on this subject in a way no one else I know can. You can help make this scholarship a reality for so many more young women than Harrison had initially envisioned."

Meaning more than just me, Juliet thought. The pain in her chest grew worse. Obviously, if Harrison wanted to soothe his conscience this way, Dorothy wasn't going to let him be so obvious about it.

"Now, come and meet my friends. And don't worry. Just be yourself, and you'll charm the pants right off them." Dorothy beamed.

Just like I did your grandson? Juliet silently asked,

as she let Dorothy tow her toward the openly curious group of society ladies.

Before Juliet could get through her first introduction, though, Nathan was bucking and snorting to get down. "Nathan," Juliet pleaded.

"Dada! Dada!" he shouted and pointed. Juliet followed his finger and saw Harrison and Ashley coming toward the veranda from around the corner of the house.

Responding to Nathan's squeal, Harrison's handsome face split into a glowing grin, and Juliet's heart clutched as she watched him squat and spread his arms wide. What would it be like to be on the receiving end of that kind of love? She'd probably keel over dead from the shock of it. Glad to the marrow of her bones that her child knew what it was like, Juliet let Nathan down off her hip, and he immediately ran for his father's arms.

"Oh, my little man," Harrison cooed after scooping the boy up and squeezing him tight against him. "Did you come to see your daddy?" he asked. Nathan pushed back from Harrison's shoulder and nodded. Harrison kissed him on the cheek. "I'm so glad. You've made me very, very happy." His warm gaze shifted to Juliet.

She couldn't meet his gaze for long. A red-hot flush engulfed her face and she looked down at her brown sandals, instead. She didn't dare let anyone see what a look from him did to her, the memories he evoked. The foolish, stupid things he made her want.

Things she couldn't have because, when all was said and done, she just wasn't good enough.

HARRISON FOUGHT to swallow past the lump that had formed in his throat when Nathan flung himself at him. His little boy's exuberant love was more than he could have ever hoped for. The part of him he couldn't seem to get a handle on wished he could elicit the same response from his baby's mother.

Juliet looked beautiful. Willowy and fair in the light summer dress that caressed her form and whispered femininity. She'd pulled her sun-kissed brown hair back into a ponytail at her nape and achieved a look of simple elegance he knew Ashley spent hundreds of dollars and countless hours in pursuit of.

As if knowing she'd stepped into his thoughts in an unfavorable light, Ashley spoke up. "My goodness, she cleans up nicely. Just imagine what a day at Saks with my charge card could do for her."

Harrison set Nathan down at his feet, his brain unable to imagine anything save the image of Juliet "cleaning up." All covered in suds and glistening heat…

"Did you know she would be here today?"

Harrison blinked and looked at his sister. "No, I didn't. When Grandmother suggested involving Juliet in the scholarship program as a way to get her to accept one herself, I assumed we'd have her work on recruiting recipients, not donors." Harrison ran a hand through his hair as he noted who was present. They represented some of the deepest and most influential pockets in the region. "What could Grandmother be thinking? Juliet can't handle this. Did *you* know about her being here today?"

Ashley shook her head, her thick, gold hoop earrings glinting in the sunlight. "Wish I had. Juliet definitely needs to go shopping."

He looked back to Juliet on the veranda, twining

her hands together nervously. "She doesn't need to go shopping, she needs to gain some confidence. If she had a little more confidence she wouldn't be so afraid of change. She'd be more willing to take the steps needed to give Nathan a better life." So Harrison wouldn't have to be forced to take those steps for her.

"I know nothing gives me confidence like a new pair of shoes," she sighed eloquently.

He made an exasperated noise at his sister's idea of personal growth and looked down at his son who'd discovered the tassels on Harrison's shoes and was doing his darnedest to pull one off. "I'm afraid it's going to take more than new clothes to reverse the damage done by her circumstances."

"You'd be surprised, Harrison." She tapped a manicured nail against her chin as she looked at Juliet speculatively.

The last thing he needed was Ashley trying to convince Juliet to change her look at the same time he was trying to get her to change her future. "Ashley," he warned.

"What?" she asked innocently.

"Promise me you won't meddle." Taking Nathan's hand, he headed for the veranda.

Behind him his sister said, "I don't meddle, dear, I *manage*."

After running the gamut of his grandmother's friends who acted as if they'd never seen such an adorable toddler in their lives, Harrison and Nathan moved to stand behind Juliet. Though she didn't acknowledge him, Harrison knew she was aware of his presence by the way she shifted on her feet, something she did often when he was around.

A glass of iced tea now clutched in her hands, Juliet was in the process, with his grandmother's occasional prompting, of tentatively explaining how the birth of an unplanned child could disrupt a young woman's plans for the future—without using herself as an example.

He wondered if, when she'd hatched this garden party scheme, his grandmother had considered what a blow it would be to Juliet's pride. She didn't want to be pitied.

But she comported herself with such subtle grace and tempered honesty that Harrison reluctantly acknowledged the warmth swelling in his chest as pride. The approving nods and smiles the older ladies sent her told him Juliet was well on her way to impressing them, also.

After standing there with Nathan playing in and out between his legs, listening to Juliet convince the knot of women around her how a college education would elevate a young woman out of hopelessness into a world of choices and possibilities, realization hit him.

Juliet was desperately trying to convince herself, also. And she was doing it with an amazing amount of class. Maybe getting her to accept the scholarship wasn't going to be so difficult, after all.

Not used to being ignored by his mother, their son chose that particular moment to test Harrison's latest observation about her class by lifting the back of Juliet's dress and tenting it over himself.

"Oh, hello!" Juliet exclaimed, and put a restraining hand on the new lump in the back of her skirt.

"Sorry," Harrison apologized on a laugh and started to reach a hand under her dress to extract Nathan, but his grandmother's discreet cough brought

him up short. Though not before several eyebrows
went up and speculative looks were exchanged
around the circle.

Just what he needed. His grandmother's friends
used these charity functions as a means to gather and
disseminate gossip. They were worse than a coffee
klatch. It wouldn't be long before the whole state of
Oregon knew that not only did the heir to the Rivers
fortune have an illegitimate child, he tried to cop a
feel off the kid's mother in public. Definitely not what
he needed when he was trying to win the board's
confidence.

Not liking his body's response to the notion of feeling up Juliet any more than losing the board's approval, Harrison withdrew his hand and stepped back.

The blush that had been riding high on Juliet's
cheeks since she'd begun talking to the other ladies
spread down her throat. "Nathan, come out of there,
please," she urged in a strained voice and ushered the
toddler from beneath her dress. But not before Harrison got an eyeful of her long, tanned legs. While
he'd seen that much, and more, before, the illicitness
of the glimpse made swallowing difficult again.

Needing to escape before the potent combination
of his desire for Juliet and being so damn proud of
her threatened his determination not to care too much,
Harrison snagged Nathan's hand. "Would it be all
right if I take him down to play on the swing?"

Juliet turned a puzzled gaze to the back lawn.

"You can't see it from here, but that big oak tree,
the one in the middle, has a wooden swing hung on
the back side." He frowned. "At least it used to."
He looked to his grandmother.

She smiled and nodded. "The swing is still there,

dear. And it's trustworthy. I was on it myself yesterday.''

The other ladies laughed, but Harrison didn't doubt her.

Juliet smiled. "Sure. That sounds like fun." She sounded wistful.

He didn't blame her for wanting to escape. Talking people out of their money, even for a great cause, was rarely fun and never easy. Especially when she didn't have a clue about how it was done and clearly doubted her abilities at every turn.

Thinking she deserved a reprieve more than his hormones deserved a rest, he leaned toward her to keep his words private. "Come join us when you get the chance. I'd like to show you the rest of the grounds."

Her smile was shy, almost tentative. "Thanks. I'd like that."

Unfortunately, so would he. At least the part of him that reveled in her ability to make him forget everything but the sunshine and the peace of just being.

And that afternoon, while playing with his child under the oak tree he'd grown up beneath, he had to remind himself not to consider why.

Chapter Eight

Juliet rubbed her damp palms on her hips as she crossed the expanse of lawn toward the oak tree where Harrison waited, her nervousness on the rise again. She'd actually relaxed a little talking to the old gals as soon as she'd realized they weren't going to eat her alive. She'd even been given the impression they liked her.

She practiced Dorothy's *pish*.

Mrs. Jacobson, Mrs. Dr. William Wheeler and the rest of the matrons probably just had better manners than the type of people Juliet was used to. Whatever the reason, she couldn't say she'd hated chatting with them. Go figure.

The thought of meeting Harrison under the old oak tree had her hands sweating again, though. While she should be suspicious of his motives, she couldn't help thinking, even hoping, that he really wanted to show her his home, to spend time with her.

Lord, she was an idiot. But she couldn't help the hope seeping through her. The sight of him chasing Nathan down the lawn, giving him gentle pushes on the swing and playing hide and seek around the tree's huge trunk until Nathan squealed had yanked at her heart unmercifully. She'd looked toward them so often the ladies finally shooed her away to go join father and son.

They were back playing on the swing, and Juliet clasped her hands together to get a grip on her emotions as she approached them. Harrison's endless appeal to her senses didn't help. His play-tousled hair and time-of-his-life grin made him look more handsome than she could have ever imagined her wayward knight looking. And while it took none of his ample strength to propel the swing, every time the thick muscles in his arms and back bunched in preparation of being called upon, she yearned to be wrapped in his strong embrace.

Talk about needing a reality check. She couldn't forget she didn't belong here. She never would.

Harrison gave Nathan a soft push on the swing and looked to her with a smile. "I see you finally got away. I'd started to think we were going to have to rescue you."

She returned his smile and propped a hand on the rough, flaky bark of the old tree, reminding herself of their game of hide-and-seek in front of the store. Her cheeks grew hot. "Thanks, but I didn't need rescuing."

His expression turned serious. "Really?"

"Yes, really. It was...not bad. Not bad at all. Actually okay. Dorothy helped me say what needed to be said, and the other women...well, they were pretty nice."

"I have to warn you, sometimes *nice* is nothing more than impeccable manners learned through years of garden parties and fund-raisers."

She narrowed her eyes at him and gave her head a

skeptical tilt. "So you're saying those ladies aren't really nice?"

"Oh, no, that's not what I mean at all," he amended. "You probably won't meet a sweeter bunch than Grandmother's friends. They do an amazing amount of work for several local and national charities." He met her gaze. "What I'm saying is, to successfully achieve your goals in this world you've got to learn to have enough confidence that it won't matter to you whether someone is nice or simply very well mannered."

"Okaaay." She drew the word out, unable to get past the fact that when he said *this world,* she knew he really meant *his world.* A world she would never have enough confidence to succeed in, no matter how many old ladies liked her.

"High, Dada. High," Nathan urged from the swing.

"Are you sure, buddy?" Harrison asked, still giving the swing gentle pushes.

"High." Nathan let go of one of the ropes and pointed to the sky.

Harrison chuckled and looked to Juliet with a brow raised. "What do you think, Mom?"

His reminder of the family unit that would never be poked yet another hole in her sorry heart. She sighed and shook her head. "The child has no fear. Or sense. He really scares me sometimes."

Harrison's expression sobered. "But I'm sure you keep a close eye on him."

His questioning tone bugged her. Pushing off the tree and crossing her arms in front of her chest, she said firmly, "Yes. I do."

He nodded once as if to close the subject and gave

her an apologetic smile. Grabbing the swing's ropes, he brought Nat to an easy halt. ''Want to go for a walk, Nathan?''

Nathan lunged off the swing in answer.

Harrison turned to her and offered his hand. ''Come on. I'd like to show you where I grew up.'' Before Juliet could decide whether or not to take his hand, he withdrew it with a glance past her shoulder at the guest-filled veranda. His cheeks looked flushed beneath his tan.

Had he forgotten himself? Or remembered who she was?

Juliet pressed her crossed arms tighter against the pain in her heart as she watched Harrison. When would she stop hurting over this guy?

When I'm dead and in my grave, she thought acidly.

His gaze still focused on the people behind her, he reached up and broke a twig off the oak tree as if that was what he'd intended to do all along.

Shifting his deep-river gaze back to hers, he nodded toward a path beside them. ''Come on,'' he whispered, an almost tired-looking smile touching the edges of his mouth.

She was about to tell him what he could do with his little tour and that it was time for her and Nathan to go, but his deep voice stopped her.

''Juliet. Let me show you my home.''

Though it hurt like hell, she still wanted to be with him. She wanted to catch a glimpse of something that would tell her who the real Harrison was. The man who snapped at people on the phone, or the man afraid of the pain from loving too much?

Knowing she shouldn't, but using Nathan's desire

to continue playing at "Rivers Park" as an excuse, Juliet uncrossed her arms and followed him.

He headed them toward a path leading to a break in the hedge wall at the back of the huge yard. Nathan alternated between running ahead of them and galloping in circles around them. He'd sleep for a week after this.

When they reached the hedge, the yard sloped down significantly and the path meandered back and forth until it disappeared from sight. She pointed at the raked-gravel path. "Where does this go?"

"To the river."

She rolled her eyes. "Of course. Us bumpkins from the boonies aren't the only ones lucky enough to squat some prime river-front property."

He didn't laugh.

She cleared her throat and wished for that rewind button again. Rubbing his nose in how different they were was not the way to get to know him. "Let's not go all the way down to the river, though, okay? Nathan loves the water, but he can't swim. I'd just as soon not have to go wading in after him."

"I hadn't planned on taking you any farther than the crest, right up here."

She followed him to the point where the slope fell away, and her breath caught at the beauty of the view. There were no blackberry bushes or birch trees to compete with, and the manicured grass grew right up to the water's edge below them. Not a single big, dumb rock in sight. Only a cute little dock complete with its own comfy-looking wooden chair. She would think she'd died and gone to heaven if she ever got to sit and watch the river from such an incredible spot.

He pointed at the dock with the twig he'd snapped

from the oak tree and put words to her thoughts. "That's where *I* escaped things. I used to come down here and sit in that Adirondack and watch the river."

She looked at his handsome profile and her heart ached for him, with the deep feelings he refused to embrace. Too bad she wasn't the woman to show him how. "Used to?"

"No time now."

Juliet muttered, "Well, duh," and fought the urge to spout *with corporations to run, illegitimate children to claim, unwed mothers to manage…* Instead, she said, "Speaking of which, we should head back." She caught Nathan on one of his circular passes and herded him back up the path. Harrison followed along beside her in silence.

Trying desperately to think of something to take her attention off his warm, muscular arm occasionally bumping against her own, Juliet asked the first question that popped into her head. "How old is this place, anyway?"

"About forty years old. My grandfather had it built. He wanted all of his family close to him."

She looked up at the big house coming into sight and raised her brows. "He must have had a huge family."

Harrison finally laughed, and she felt its rumbly warmth clear to her toes. "No, my father was an only child, as was his father."

"Is that why your company is named Two Rivers? Because it was run by your dad and grandpa?"

"No. They built the plant near where the McKenzie flows into the Willamette."

"Ah. Two rivers. Gotcha."

He laughed again, and his shoulder brushed firmly

against hers. Juliet nearly cried with wanting more. More of his touch. More of him. She couldn't have either.

"Grandfather built the house so big because he wanted my dad to continue living here after he married and had a family of his own."

"Which consists of you and your sister."

"Yes. Now it's just me and my sister."

His tone hinted at a pain she knew all too well. She still missed her grandfather so much, especially now, when she could use a strong, sympathetic shoulder to lean on. A shoulder that didn't belong to a glorious man she could never have. "I'm sorry about your mother, Harrison."

He merely grunted in response. Apparently, he didn't want to talk about her. Juliet could understand that, too. A confident, rule-the-world kind of guy like Harrison probably couldn't handle being brought down by something like grief, the one thing in the world he truly could not control.

She kept her gaze on the fine gravel of the path, afraid to look at him and risk losing the battle she had to wage to keep from throwing her arms around him and comfort him until he healed. She should be worrying about healing herself, not him.

Thinking it wise to change the subject to something she knew made him happy, she asked, "So, what's running a huge company like?"

"A lot of hard work, but worth the effort."

"Worth the effort because it makes you the big bucks?" She noticed he stopped tapping the twig against his leg. Bringing up money probably wasn't the best idea. Good Lord, what if he thought she was as money-grubbing as her mom, after all?

He continued walking for a step or two before he answered. "Worth it because it's challenging. Exhilarating. And did I mention a lot of hard work?"

She could hear the smile in his voice and couldn't keep from looking up and meeting his grin with one of her own, her relief intense because he hadn't taken her comment the wrong way. "So you like hard work. I suppose that explains why the door didn't hit you in the rear the second you found out about Nathan."

He stopped and looked at her. "Accepting Nathan into my life was the right thing to do."

Meeting his gaze dead-on, she asked, "And that's the only reason? Because it's the right thing?"

He watched Nathan playing on a stone bench next to the path ahead of them for a moment, then shook his head. "No, not at all. Nathan makes my heart soar. He did from the very second I realized he was mine. I think about him all the time and I want to be with him." He turned and looked her in the eye again. His voice thick, he whispered, "I *want* him in my life."

Overwhelmed by the familiar drowning sensation, she had to work hard to breathe, unsure if it was from desperation or joy for her child.

Making a mother's sacrifice by putting her son first, she whispered back, "I won't ever keep you from him, Harrison. He deserves to have *you* in *his* life."

His green eyes darkened with emotion. "I'm glad to hear that, Juliet. Very, very glad." He reached out and tucked a blowing strand of hair that had escaped her ponytail behind her ear, his finger trailing along her cheek the entire way.

Juliet closed her eyes against the heat and yearning

left behind. Two emotions she apparently would be bosom buddies with from now on.

His fingers lingering in the hair behind her ear, he asked, "Will you accept the scholarship?"

She groaned and pulled away. She couldn't do this, couldn't play this torturous game. "I don't want your charity, Harrison. Why can't you understand that?"

He blew out a noisy breath. "The only thing I can't understand is why you're being so stubborn. Why won't you let me help you?"

"Because then I would just be something else you were the boss of. Something else you controlled."

"Good God, Juliet. Controlling you is the last thing I could ever do." He tossed away the twig. "How can I control you when I can't even control my feelings for you?"

Stunned, Juliet met his gaze. The heat in his eyes made her knees weak and the air too thick to breathe. She wanted to step closer and let that warmth invade her body and fill all the empty spaces she endured, the biggest one in her heart.

She swayed toward him, pulled by the same unseen force that always drew her to him. Despite all their differences, she felt such a strong connection to him.

Woman to man.

Soul to soul.

He bent his head and she met his kiss halfway. His mouth moved gently over hers, coaxing her to open for him with a sweetness that battered her heart even more. The instant she parted her lips he made a rumbling sound and settled his mouth firmly on hers. Heat flooded her and she reached up to grab the front of his shirt to further anchor herself to him. He responded by running his hands from her bare elbows to the tops of her arms, then gripped her there as if he couldn't decide whether to pull her closer or push her away.

Nothing else mattered when Harrison looked at her, touched her, kissed her. Nothing but moving close enough to feel a part of him. She wanted to climb right inside and live in his skin.

But to be a part of him she would have to be a part of his world, and that wasn't possible.

Anger surged through her again and gave strength to her limbs. He had no business doing this to her, to them. She made the decision for him and stepped back, breaking the kiss and leaving her heart in the gravel at his feet.

She glared at him as she struggled to regain her breath. "So you can't control your feelings for me? Well, it's past time for you to try."

HARRISON FOUGHT to calm his pounding heart as he watched Juliet and Nathan walk back to the house, the gentle breeze sabotaging his efforts by forming the thin material of her dress to her slender hips and thighs. He cursed and scooped up the stick he'd played with to keep his hands off her. Fat lot of good that'd done. He *had* been trying to control his feelings for her.

Trying damn hard.

Nothing he'd tried so far worked, and it wasn't simply because she wouldn't accept his *charity*. He just couldn't shake the pull she had on him, both physical and—damn it—emotional. And the fact that she continued to kiss him back only muddied the water further. Maybe he wasn't the only one fighting something. Did she still feel the connection after all?

"I do *not* need this right now," he grumbled, and headed off in Juliet and Nathan's wake.

His son's exuberant hopping and Juliet's angry pace forced Harrison to lengthen his stride so it wouldn't look like she had stormed away from him to the curious observers on the veranda. Though he hung back enough to give her and himself space. What the hell could he say to her, anyhow? She was right. He just didn't know what to do about his crazy, conflicting feelings.

When they reached the veranda, Juliet, without looking at Harrison, picked Nathan up to keep him from escaping back toward the oak tree, then made her way to his grandmother who stood chatting with two women next to the French doors to the house. He took his time climbing the steps.

She stood quietly off to the side of the small group until his grandmother was able to acknowledge her. "I'm sorry, Dorothy, but it's getting close to nap-time—"

"No nap!" Nathan exclaimed to the immense amusement of the older ladies.

Juliet ignored him and continued, "So we need to get going."

"You could put him down here," Grandmother offered with undisguised hope.

Juliet's eyes darted to Harrison as he approached, then back to his grandmother. "I think I'd better get him home to his crib."

"Oh, certainly, dear." She patted Nathan on his little back. Turning to the other women, she said, "Ladies, if you'll excuse me for a moment. I'd like to walk Juliet to the door." She looked at him and extended a hand. "Harrison, you'll join me, of course."

"Of course, Grandmother."

Juliet again only gave him the barest glance as he moved toward them, but her annoyance wasn't obvious. He hoped his annoyance with himself didn't show, either. He didn't want to explain his lack of control to his grandmother any more than he wanted to explain it to Juliet. Or himself.

He followed a step behind as his grandmother escorted Juliet and Nathan toward the front of the house, praising Juliet for her efforts in winning contributions to the scholarship fund the entire way. He found his chest filling with the swell of pride again. Damn. He really *was* out of control.

The sound of the front door slamming and his father's voice reached them just before they entered the foyer. "Donavon! My putter was *not* in my bag or at the club. Are you *sure* it isn't in my study?"

Harrison instinctively made a grab for Juliet to steer her in another direction, since she'd been through enough today without having to meet his father on top of everything, but his grandmother looped her arm through Juliet's and hailed his dad at the same instant.

Harrison could do nothing but follow them into the foyer where his father stood, having returned from his Saturday-morning golf game early and yelling at an employee who was nowhere in sight. Normally his father went on a golf marathon and played two rounds on Saturdays, so it hadn't occurred to Harrison that Juliet might have to face George Rivers today.

"George, dear," his grandmother said again, though it was clear by the frown on his father's face that they already had his attention. ''I have two some-ones here I'd like you to meet.''

Juliet glanced over her shoulder at Harrison, her apprehension plain on her lovely face and in the way his grandmother had to practically pull her forward. An urge to protect her from his grouchy father seized Harrison and he strode to her other side, placing what he hoped to be a reassuring hand on the small of her back.

His father planted his hands on his hips as they approached him. ''Good Go—''

''George,'' his grandmother cut him off, though her tone remained pleasant. ''This is your grandson, Na-than, and his mother, Juliet Jones.'' She indicated to his father and stated the obvious, ''Juliet, this is Har-rison's father, George Rivers.''

Her hands full holding Nathan, Juliet simply said, ''Hi,'' in a soft voice and nodded to his father, who in turn eyed her through narrowed lids.

Anger rose in Harrison for his father being any-thing less than civil. ''Dad—'' he started to warn, but his father shifted his attention to Harrison's son.

''So this is him?'' He inclined his head at Nathan, who returned his regard with the classic Rivers raised brow. George quirked his mouth, obviously seeing the family resemblance, then looked to Harrison. ''Doesn't look anything like you. You're positive he's yours?''

Harrison glared at him. How could his father ask such a thing when the proof stared him straight in the face?

Juliet answered for him. ''Nathan is Harrison's son, Mr. Rivers.''

Grandmother patted her on the arm. "Oh, do call him George, dear."

Juliet gave his grandmother a weak smile but it was clear she was thinking, *Yeah, right.*

His father's fists slid off his hips and he heaved a sigh. "Fabulous. Just fabulous," he muttered.

Harrison lowered his chin. If the man said another word—

His grandmother cut off the thought. "Juliet was good enough to come and speak with some of the ladies about a scholarship program we've—"

One of said ladies chose that moment to enter the foyer from the hall.

"George!" Mrs. Jacobson called out, her arms spread wide. His father complied by going to her and allowing her to hug him and kiss him on the cheek. "My, but you look more and more like your father. Doesn't he, Dorothy?"

"Yes, he does. Just as our little Nathan so closely resembles Harrison."

Harrison looked at the child who had burst into his life and his heart. His throat closed up. Despite all the turmoil, he was so thankful he'd found his son. He reached out and smoothed the angel-fine hair from Nathan's forehead. His son responded with a sweet smile before nuzzling his face against Juliet's neck. He was indeed growing sleepy in his mother's arms.

Harrison raised his gaze to Juliet's and let her see what he felt. Hopefully she would be reassured by his love for the child they had created. What he felt for her was an entirely different matter. One he didn't care to analyze.

Her beautiful brown eyes clouded with emotion before she looked away, and he was pretty damn sure she wasn't feeling reassured. He sighed. Emotions run amok caused nothing but problems.

Mrs. Jacobson released his father and wagged a finger at Harrison. "Potent genes, I'm thinking."

Feeling the embarrassment roll off Juliet in waves, Harrison changed the subject. "Was there something you needed from your car, Mrs. Jacobson? I'd be happy to get it for you."

She waved him off and started for the door. "You dear boy. No, I'm afraid I must be going. Thank you for inviting me, Dorothy. Good works, as usual, my dear. Good works. I will see you later, I'm sure. Tuesday, to be exact."

Grandmother laughed and nodded. "That's right. Tuesday at the museum."

Donavon emerged from his small office at the back of the foyer and reached the door at the perfect time to open it for Mrs. Jacobson. She paused on the threshold and turned back to look at them. "And George, congratulations on the two wonderful additions to your family." She pointed at Nathan and Juliet. "You must be so proud. Good day to you all."

Harrison thought he heard his father make a rude noise, but he refused to acknowledge him as he watched Donavon close the door behind Mrs. Jacobson. His father would just have to find a way to deal with the situation.

Next to him, Juliet shifted, then stepped toward Donavon and whispered, "Um, could you please get the diaper bag for me?"

Donavon smiled at her, obviously charmed by her tentativeness. "Certainly. I'll be but a moment."

"Thanks tons." Juliet stayed by the door with her

gaze diverted, lulling Nathan asleep by swaying back and forth.

His grandmother cleared her throat. "Well, I should return to the rest of my guests." But first she went to Juliet. "Thank you for coming, dear. You did wonderfully."

Juliet shrugged, but a shy smile lifted the corners of her lush mouth.

The older woman patted her arm. "I'm sure I'll speak with you soon." She leaned forward and kissed Nathan on the back of his head. He barely stirred. "Goodbye, my precious angel."

Harrison watched Juliet as her gaze remained on his grandmother's retreating back, then she glanced from his father to Harrison, her expression guarded. Harrison looked at his father and found suspicion plain on his face. Damn him for not even trying to be civil.

Donavon reemerged with the diaper bag in one hand and Juliet's keys and his father's putter in the other. He paused in front of George. "It was out back on the practice green," Donavon said evenly, his patience legendary. He handed his father the putter, who was slow taking it, his attention for some reason on the keys.

When he was free of the golf club, Donavon brought the bag and keys to Juliet. Harrison reached for the diaper bag, intending to walk her to her car and say...something, but his father's voice stopped him.

"Harrison, I need to speak with you for a moment."

"As soon as I help Juliet get Nathan into his car seat."

Juliet finally spoke. "No, I'm fine. Really. You go talk to your dad. I don't need any help." She hoisted Nathan higher on her hip to free a hand, and allowed Donavon to slip the bag's long strap onto her shoulder.

Harrison let out an exasperated breath. "But I *want* to help you."

His father butted in. "She said she was fine. I need to speak with you before I have to leave for my next foursome. I can't delay it because of a banquet I have to attend tonight."

"Go ahead, Harrison," Juliet insisted. "I'm a pro at this."

"I'll assist her," Donavon offered as he opened the front door.

His father said, "There, she's taken care of. Now, come with me." He turned and went into his study, obviously assuming Harrison would comply.

Harrison wasn't in the mood. He started to follow Juliet out the door, but she stopped and gave him a pleading look. She whispered, "You should go talk to him."

"I don't need to talk to him. He has his opinions, and I don't agree with them. No amount of talking will change that."

She closed her eyes for a moment and took a deep breath. When she opened them she met his gaze directly. "Then you should try to change his opinions. For Nathan's sake." Without waiting for a reply, she turned and hurried down the steps.

He wanted to talk about their kiss, but seeing her wisdom, he said, "I'll call you later." Frustration made his tone curt.

She didn't acknowledge him or stop on her way to

Willie's old truck, looking sorely out of place amongst the luxury sedans.

"Harrison," his dad yelled from the study, and for Nathan's sake he decided to heed the call.

George Rivers had taken up his position of power behind the huge desk, but it'd been a long time since Harrison had been intimidated by the image his father presented. He knew too well how the man's mind worked.

Harrison came to a stop right in front of the desk, crossed his arms over his chest and returned his father's glare. He absolutely refused to compromise over anything involving Nathan.

"Just how well do you know your child's mother?"

Harrison blinked. He'd expected his dad to start out berating him for parading his illegitimate child in front of such an influential crowd. He hadn't expected Juliet to come up first. Had his father seen them kissing?

Fighting the flush he felt creeping up his neck, Harrison answered, "I'm getting to know her. I think I have a pretty good idea about the type of person she is and what motivates her."

"Do you." It wasn't a question. "I happen to think I have a pretty good idea about the type of person who would choose to carry their keys on a miniature beer can key chain."

Harrison pulled his brows down. He hadn't noticed her keys. Then the explanation dawned on him. "Those weren't her keys. She'd driven her brother's truck, so I'm certain that's his key chain."

His father didn't look impressed. He leaned his elbows on the desk and tented his fingers. "Does this brother of hers live with Juliet and your son?"

Harrison fought the urge to shift his weight. He knew the train of thought his dad was on, and an uncomfortable prickling started at the base of his neck because he'd ridden that train himself. "Yes, he does."

"So your child is being reared in a beer-can-key-chain culture. Are you satisfied with this?"

Harrison blew out another exasperated breath at his dad for hitting right on the mark and dropped his hands to his hips. "No, I'm not satisfied with Nathan's present environment, and I'm taking steps to encourage Juliet to make some changes."

"So these *steps* do not include legally removing your son from that environment?"

"I'm not going to take Nathan away from his mother."

"Why not?"

"Because she's a good mother," he grated. Lord, she'd given up her dreams for Nathan.

Slowing rising to his feet, his dad fixed him with a hard look. "Are you sure?"

Harrison crossed his arms over his chest again. "Yes, I'm sure."

"You mean, as sure as you can be after knowing her for only a short time."

The pride he'd felt for her today and the way she pulled at him emotionally despite his best defense made his conviction ring true. "I'm sure, Dad. Juliet is a good person and a great mother. I trust her. Once she gains some confidence in herself and allows me to help her, Nathan's environment will improve. End of discussion.'' Harrison turned to leave, hoping he could catch Juliet and tell her just that.

''I hope you are right, son. Because I unequivocally believe environment determines everything.''

Harrison left the study, shaking his head at his dad's stubbornness. Stubbornness Harrison had inherited his fair share of. Obviously, there was a lot to be said for nature, too. Fortunately for Juliet and Nathan, Harrison intended to put his stubbornness to a good use.

He opened the front door and scanned the drive for Willie's truck, but Juliet had already left. He blew out a pressure-relieving breath. He'd have to bring up the discussion of nature versus nurture with her another time—tomorrow would be soon enough—and hopefully she wouldn't still be angry at him over his inability to keep himself in check.

Maybe his own anger at his lack of control would be enough to put an end to the problem once and for all. Unfortunately, wanting Juliet seemed to be a part of his nature, too.

Chapter Nine

While Nathan played contentedly with his bear on the bedroom floor behind her, Juliet focused on what she could see of the river from her balcony, but found no peace. She doubted she'd ever reach that simple state of being again. Not now. Not when she knew. She'd tried to deny it. She'd tried to refuse it. She'd tried to ignore it. But she couldn't. She had to face the facts.

She loved Harrison Rivers and it was beginning to look like he had feelings for her, too. But she could never be with him, because she would never fit into his world and he knew it.

Life sucked.

She'd always thought she was smarter than the rest of them. But she wasn't. She was just as stupid, making all the wrong choices.

All the way home from the Rivers Estate she'd tried to convince herself it didn't have to be this way; she didn't have to give in to his seductive presence again. But his eyes, his gentleness, his touch made her realize she was doomed.

She propped her elbows on her knees and held her head in her hands, staring unseeingly at the weathered boards beneath her bare feet. What was Harrison thinking? He had to have seen how constipated his dad looked when Dorothy had introduced him to her and Nathan on their way out.

Especially after Mrs. Jacobson strolled in and let him know what a charming addition she thought Juliet and Nathan were to the Rivers family. He didn't look too hip on having ''white trash'' littering his family tree.

She sat up straight in the chair and squared her shoulders. No way was she going to start thinking like Willie. She and Nathan were the ones who were too good. The Riverses didn't deserve them.

She gave a harsh laugh. Yeah, refusing to darken his ornate doorstep would really show old George Rivers. Her shoulders slumped. The only one who would suffer if she cut contact with that family was Nathan. He was as much in love with Harrison as she was.

In frustration, Juliet bunched the skirt of her good dress in her fists.

She would suffer no matter what choice she made, but Nathan was the only one who mattered.

''Hi,'' Nathan chirped as he came out onto the balcony with her.

Relaxing her fists, she released her dress. ''Hi, baby.''

He moved to the edge of the balcony and leaned against the railing. ''Dada play-play-play,'' he said with a pleased smile on his precious face.

''Yes, he did, baby,'' she answered, her attention focusing again on the image of Harrison's heart-melting, soft smile in her mind's eye. Out of habit she said, ''Move back from the rail, bab—''

The sound of cracking wood cut her off, and she jerked her head in time to see Nathan's little body falling backward through the separating railing.

"Nathan!" she screamed and lunged out of her chair.

HARRISON ABSENTLY WHISTLED through his teeth as he headed for the door to his father's study, intent on borrowing the spare cell phone kept in the desk to replace the broken one in his hand. The stupid things really didn't like to be drop-kicked more than a couple of times. He was about to shove the partially open door wide when the sound of his father's voice coming from inside stopped him.

"You said yourself the place is falling to pieces. It was only a matter of time before something like this happened."

An uneasy chill raced up his spine. Harrison pushed the door the rest of the way open and entered the room. His father, dressed in black formal wear for the banquet he was to attend that night, stood with a hip propped against the huge desk and Harrison's grandmother paced before him wringing her hands, her normally perfect hair slightly mussed as if she'd been running her hands through it.

The chill settled in his stomach. "What are you two talking about?"

Grandmother turned. "Oh, Harrison, there you are. Thank heaven." She hurried toward him, her delicate hands outstretched. "I've been trying to reach you for the past hour."

He took one of her hands with his free one and raised the busted phone he held in the other. "I went to the office to pick up some work. My cell phone's on the blink,'' he said. Looking down into eyes darkened by worry and the forest-green pantsuit she wore, he drew his brows together, ''Why? What's wrong?''

''Darling, there seems to have been an accident. But I have been in constant contact with the hospital, and they have assured me he's fine. It's just that Juliet was so upset when she called looking for you—''

The chill in Harrison's gut turned to fear and exploded throughout his body. His questions came out in a rush. ''Juliet? Is it Nathan? He's hurt? What happened? Where is he?''

''Yes, it's Nathan, but they're nearly certain—''

His father raised his hands sharply in the air. ''Good grief, Mother. Don't you think you've got the boy worked up enough as it is?'' George Rivers pushed off from the desk and approached them. ''Harrison, for that child's sake you have to sue for custody. Apparently Nathan fell and hit his head. Juliet had him taken to Sacred Heart Hospital by ambulance to be checked out—''

Harrison didn't hear any more. He turned and ran for his car. Fear for his son nearly blinded him and he choked on its taste.

Oh, God. He couldn't lose Nathan. Not when he'd only just found him. And Juliet. Dear Lord, she'd be devastated.

He raced to the hospital as fast as possible, breaking more traffic laws than he had in his whole life, and blasted into the emergency room waiting area. He found Juliet doubled over on an orange couch, her mother and brother on either side of her. Phyllis and Willie seemed to actually be trying to comfort her. Willie was holding Juliet's hand while Phyllis patted her back and muttered a lot of there-theres and hush-nows.

Willie spotted him first. Relief replaced the look of helplessness he wore instead of his usual smirk. "Finally. The cavalry's here."

"Juliet," Harrison rasped.

She raised her forehead off her knees. Her normally sun-kissed face was pale, but for the red splotches riding high on her cheeks from crying. And instead of seeing sanctuary in her eyes, Harrison saw a misery only a mother could feel.

Or a father.

He opened his arms to her. Without hesitation she launched herself at him and wrapped her arms tightly around his neck. He spread his hands over her back and held her against him, giving and getting comfort all in the same moment.

"Oh, Harrison," she sobbed. Feeling her wet cheek against his, Harrison's heart twisted and fear strangled him more than her tight grip ever could.

Though dreading the answer, he had to ask, "Nathan?"

Willie answered for her. "He's fine. The doc said he just got his little bell rung, but she won't believe him. Making them do every test known to man on the kid." Exasperation tinged his words. "She was putting up such a stink they made her wait out here."

Relief surged through Harrison. Despite Willie's often callous behavior, Harrison believed Willie loved his nephew, and if there were any cause for concern, he'd say so.

"That's right," Phyllis added. "The head doctor—"

Willie barked out a laugh and cut her off. "Meaning the neuro-whatever."

"That's what I said, the head doctor."

Willie slumped back against the couch and rolled his eyes. "It sounds like you mean the one in charge."

Juliet gulped in a breath, bringing Harrison's attention back to her. "He fell, Harrison. He fell so hard. And it was all my fault. I was only halfway paying attention and he fell. It scared him so bad. He cried and cried and cried." Juliet's whole body shook with the force of her own tears.

He tightened his hold on her. He could smell her fresh, summertime scent despite the hospital's antiseptic aroma. "It's all right for you to be scared, too, sweetheart. But you've talked to the doctor, right?"

She nodded against his cheek.

"And the doctor said Nathan's okay, right?"

Again she nodded.

He loosened his hold enough to run a soothing hand up and down her trembling back. "Shh. The doctor wouldn't lie to you, Juliet. I'll talk to him, too. Okay?"

He set her away from him and looked down into her face. The pain and regret he saw made the back of his eyes burn. He wanted to wrap her in his arms again and kiss her misery away.

But first he had to hear for himself what the neurologist had to say.

Harrison settled Juliet back on the couch between her mother and brother, then went to the emergency room check-in desk.

"Hello," he greeted the hospital-uniformed woman

seated behind the high desk. "My name is Harrison Rivers and I—"

"Oh, yes, the father of the little boy who fell." She pulled a piece of paper from a slot in a stacked organizer on her desk.

Harrison blinked and struggled to hide his surprise. He hadn't expected Juliet to name him as Nathan's father on the hospital documentation. But then a voice inside his head—one that sounded suspiciously like his father's—said she'd probably only signed his name on the "party responsible for payment" line. Harrison mentally responded that he didn't give a damn. He *was* responsible for Nathan, and he liked being acknowledged as such.

"Yes, that's right," he said. "I'd like to speak to the doctor treating Nathan, if I may."

"Most certainly." She started to get up, but stopped when a tall, thin man in green scrubs emerged through the swinging doors at the opposite end of the waiting room. "There's Dr. Menton now."

Harrison greeted the doctor and introduced himself. Behind Dr. Menton, a nurse came through the doors carrying Nathan on her hip. Aside from obvious traces of tears, Nathan looked no different from when Harrison had last seen him earlier in the day.

"Dada!" Nathan hailed him with his usual enthusiasm.

Harrison eagerly reached to take his son from the nurse, but Juliet appeared between them and gathered her baby into her arms. Harrison had no choice but to let Nathan go, though there was no mistaking the reluctance he felt. He'd suspected he wouldn't be able to control his emotions where Nathan was concerned, and he'd been right.

With an accepting sigh, he returned his attention to the doctor and grilled the man about the exam and the tests they had run.

"The CAT scan confirmed what I told the boy's mother. He has a bump on his head. That's all," Dr. Menton said. "We've given him acetaminophen for the headache he undoubtedly has, and that should also help reduce the swelling at the sight of the contusion."

The doctor gestured at Nathan. "These little ones are amazing. They can take quite a tumble, like yours did, and not be any worse for wear. It's truly a blessing they're as tough as they are. Of course, the circumstances of the fall greatly influences the outcome, and from the sound of it, the fact that Nathan landed on soft, loose dirt contributed to the positive outcome of this incident."

Harrison turned a questioning look on Juliet.

"The flower bed I dug out front," she explained.

Harrison nodded, having noticed her efforts to improve the store's appearance. The pride he'd felt for her earlier flooded his every pore. It was all he could do not to kiss her.

Dr. Menton slapped a hand on the top of Harrison's shoulder. "All said and done, you guys dodged a bullet this time. Children are pretty active at this age, and you really have to keep an eye on them." He gently chucked Nathan under the chin. "Just to be safe, rouse him every four hours or so tonight, and if you can't wake him, bring him back here. Though I'm sure he's fine. Good luck." With that Dr. Menton went back through the swinging doors.

Harrison moved next to Juliet and ran a hand up and down Nathan's little back. Juliet would only meet

his eyes for a moment, but Harrison saw the misery
that had consumed her before it dropped away, replaced by...something else. What, he wasn't sure.

Dismissing Juliet's expression, he sighed with relief that they both seemed to have recovered from the
initial scare. If Juliet became this worked up over Nathan falling down and bonking his head, he hated to
think how she would handle their son really getting
hurt. God willing, that would never happen.

"It's getting late," Harrison said. "How about if I
give you two a ride home."

Willie answered from the couch. "That'd be cool,
man." He stood and stretched. "The only rig we've
got here is my truck. It'd be a real pisser trying to fit
us all in the cab, with Booger's car seat and all."

"Willie," Juliet warned in a low voice.

"Oh, sorry, sorry. Make that, with *Nathan's* car
seat and all."

"What do you think?" Harrison asked Juliet, who
was still glaring at her brother. "Is that okay?"

"I guess. Sure. Thanks."

Harrison noticed her brevity, but considering her
upset of before, he found it understandable. He escorted them to his car while Willie ran to get the car
seat out of his truck.

"I'll see you back at home, Julie," Phyllis said and
followed after Willie.

Juliet had barely finished strapping Nathan into his
car seat before he fell sound asleep.

Harrison watched her get settled into the front passenger seat next to him and said, "It's been a rough
day for our little man."

"That's the understatement of the millennium,"
she mumbled.

He waited for her to say more, but when she didn't, he leaned toward her and ran a hand over her silky hair. "You shouldn't beat yourself up so much over this, sweetheart. Accidents happen."

He pulled a lopsided grin and touched his fingertips to the thin ridge of scar tissue gracing the underside of his chin. Though the fine, ridged line wasn't much, it was a bear to shave around. "Heck, I managed to tumble down the main staircase of our house with no less than my parents, two grandparents, a nanny and the butler looking on. Kids are hard on themselves."

She didn't respond, so he headed them out of town in silence.

They were nearly to her home when Harrison decided he wasn't ready to part with her just yet. He needed to know she was going to be okay. His chest still ached from seeing her so upset. Spying a turnout on the river's side of the road, he pulled off and shut down the engine.

Juliet looked at him questioningly so he said, "We should let Nathan sleep a little longer before we have to disturb him by getting him out of his car seat."

She glanced back at their baby, then considered Harrison for a moment before she nodded in agreement.

The sun had already set, but enough light lingered for him to see the puffiness and redness from crying that marred her beautiful eyes.

He leaned toward her and ran the back of his knuckles down her satin-smooth cheek. The feel of her skin made his blood start to percolate. "How are you doing?"

She closed her eyes and tentatively nuzzled his hand. "I'm okay. Now."

He cupped her cheek with his palm, his guts twisting with the want and need she generated in him. "Good. It tore me up to see you like that." With the gentlest touch he was capable of, Harrison ran the pad of his thumb over her luscious lips. All the blood that had been bubbling in his head raced straight to his lap. Halfway in an attempt to remind his out-of-control body what was at stake here, he vowed, "Juliet, I don't ever want to cause you that kind of pain."

"I think it's unavoidable, Harrison," she whispered against his thumb.

"Ah, Juliet," he groaned, half because of her words, half because of the tremors rampaging from his thumb to the rest of his body. Heaven help him, he wanted to taste her lips and feel her body wrapped around him again. She drew him to her in so many ways, on so many levels, it was impossible to deny his yearning for her.

When her bronzed-earth gaze dropped down to his lips, Harrison lost his battle of denial. He growled and slipped his hand into her silky hair, pulling her mouth to his. Her lips opened beneath his and welcomed his hard kiss. The sensation of her hot mouth, of her tongue sliding against his, exploded through his body and he leaned farther into her. She smelled like the river and summer and he wanted to drown in her.

She made a purring sound of need and his gut clenched in response. All he could think of was touching her, conveying his own need for her until she wanted him as much, too. So she wouldn't doubt him. So she would trust him. Like their first time.

He found the hem of her dress and dragged it up her leg until he reached her upper thigh, her skin so smooth and soft it made the material of her dress seem coarse. Still kissing her sweet mouth, he brushed his fingertips between her thighs until she parted them for him with a moaned invitation.

His blood roaring in his ears, he accepted the invitation and slipped his hand between her legs and found her wet heat.

Whispering his name against his lips, she sunk her hands in his hair and lifted her hips against his caressing touch, urging him to stroke her harder, deeper.

He made love to her with his hand, with his mouth on hers, raw need pushing him on. His thumb rubbed and his fingers stroked and dipped until she ground down on his hand. He wanted to exist with her in this moment, in this place, for eternity.

She cried out and the exquisite tremors racking her seeped into his body and sent his heart soaring. The only other times in his life he'd ever felt this way had been with this woman. With Juliet.

The sound of shuffling in the back seat made her yank away from him like she'd been hit. Her eyes were huge, and it took several blinks before she could clear the traces of passion from them.

She pulled in a shaky breath. "I thought you said you didn't want to hurt me?" she rasped.

He couldn't think. "Juliet, I—"

"My God, Harrison. What are you trying to do to me? What do you want from me? Everything? You've already got it. You're already everywhere. You're in my head so much I can hardly think anymore." She blinked and a great big, fat tear rolled down her cheek. "God," she sobbed softly, "I was thinking about you when Nathan fell from the balcony today."

Her words hit him like a bucket of ice-cold water,

washing away his confusion, passion and regrets. ''What?''

She pulled back yet farther and pressed herself against the passenger door, looking everywhere but at him.

He reached for her and grabbed her shoulders. *''Nathan fell from the balcony?''*

She started to cry harder. ''He's never allowed to get close to the railing, but I was thinking about you, and he was talking about you, and he started pushing against the rails—''

Harrison shook his head, the image of his baby falling from the second-story balcony onto the ground below filling him with rage and horror. ''You let Nathan out on that damn, dilapidated balcony?'' He let go of her in disbelief. ''I trusted you.''

Chapter Ten

Harrison drove to Juliet's family's store too angry to form a coherent thought, let alone speak.

He'd trusted her. Trusted her to be a good mother to his son. But she had been careless and negligent. Good Lord, the emergency room doctor could have reported her to Children's Services.

His father had been right. Environment did dictate everything. He pulled the car up in front of the door and slammed the gearshift into park.

Huddled in the seat next to him, Juliet asked in a small voice, "Harrison?"

He looked up at the balcony, noticing the missing slats and ground his teeth together. It was a wonder Nathan hadn't been killed. "How could you have let him out on that rickety thing?" He looked at her. "I trusted you to be a competent caregiver."

Her expression turned bewildered. "But you said accidents happen. Like your chin."

"Falling down some stairs is a lot different from falling off a dangerous, second-story balcony." He flung the car door open and climbed out, then took considerably more care opening the rear passenger door.

"What are you doing?"

He leaned in and gently unbuckled his precious son. "I'm going to take Nathan up to bed, because that's the best thing for him tonight. But I want you to stay where you are because I'm not done talking to you about this." He lifted the sleeping baby from his car seat and cradled Nathan's head against his shoulder, careful not to touch his bump.

He strode to the store holding his child tight to his chest, the thought of what could have happened making his stomach curdle. He had never felt this scared before. Even when he'd seen how sick his mother was, had accepted that she would indeed die, he hadn't been as frightened. He'd been so angry he wanted to rage at the world, then so hurt he'd needed to run away for a while, but not this scared.

And he needed to lash out. But at Juliet? She was only human. Only human and living in an unsafe place. Still, he'd trusted her.

He walked through the dark store and into the living area, his gaze flicking over the irregular, dark shapes in the room. He didn't need the lights on to know most of them were piles of unfolded laundry or other junk that would never get put away. Though Juliet had made a tremendous effort to clean the place lately, with two lazy relatives messing it up right behind her, there was no way she could stay on top of things and be an attentive mother to his son at the same time.

Harrison felt sick to his stomach. No matter her intentions, Juliet couldn't win. And here he was, jumping on the bandwagon. He paused at the bottom of the stairs at the sight of Willie and Phyllis sitting around the small kitchen table.

The startled expressions on their faces made him think he'd interrupted something. It probably somehow involved him, or his money, and their plans to separate it from him.

He didn't give a damn.

Without a word he started up the stairs. The glow of a night-light led him to the correct door, and he pushed it open gently. The room was small and smelled of baby lotion and summer. He ruthlessly slapped down his body's response to Juliet's scent. Though all of the available wall space was taken up by a whitewashed dresser, a very nice-looking crib and a twin bed, the room was entirely free of clutter. A very different picture from the rest of the house.

Even in the soft glow of a bunny lamp set atop the dresser he could see how clean and tidy the room was kept. He'd go so far as to say it was decorated, with scraps of lace and homemade-looking stuffed creatures here and there.

So this was Juliet's space. As different from the rest of the place as she was from the rest of her family. But Nathan couldn't be raised entirely in such a small room, and Harrison hardened his resolve again. He had to move Nathan out of here. If he'd been able to control himself around Juliet he would have had Nathan safe at the estate long before this happened.

He went to the crib and laid Nathan down, thankful he'd remained asleep, and was about to place a soft kiss on his son's cheek when a loud *thunk* coming from out front stopped him. It sounded again, drawing him downstairs and toward the store to investigate. The third whack rattled the whole storefront.

He pushed open the door and froze at the sight of Juliet standing below the balcony. She held a sledgehammer in her hands. Rearing back, she took a swing at the closest post supporting the balcony. She was trying to knock the whole thing down.

"Juliet!" he called and started toward her, but her wild backswing kept him back.

She let out an enormous sob in response. Even in the faint light he could see she was distraught.

"Juliet," he soothed, trying to grab the sledgehammer.

"No," she snapped and swung the hammer out of his reach. "I have to take it down." She took another swing.

Whack.

"It has to come down," she gritted out.

Whack.

"Should of come down a long time ago. I knew it wasn't safe, but it was my spot."

Whack.

"My spot." She started crying in earnest again, the way she had at the hospital. "I thought he'd be safe if he stayed back, but he didn't stay back. I should have known. You're right. It was my fault."

Whack.

"My fault!" she cried.

Harrison's heart, pitiful knot that it was, felt torn from his chest. She was willing to sacrifice her favorite place on earth for their child. She loved their baby so much. She would never purposefully do anything to harm Nathan. Harrison had grown up in the best of environments and he'd still been hurt. Accidents did happen. And Juliet shouldn't be blamed for something every parent faces.

"Juliet. Please, honey, stop." Harrison darted a hand out and snatched the sledgehammer from her grip. "If that thing comes crashing down, you could get hurt."

"I want it down."

She tried to grab the hammer's handle back but he held it up out of her reach. She jumped in an attempt to grasp it, so he tossed the thing away from them and wrapped his arms tight around her.

"Harrison, ple-ease," she sobbed, and squirmed in his embrace.

"Shh, sweetheart," he whispered into her hair. "This isn't the way."

"But the...balcony...*dangerous,*" she said between great gulps of air. *"This whole place..."*

Harrison couldn't believe she was echoing his concerns. It would be so easy to tell her Nathan should come home with him—so he'd be safe. She'd undoubtedly agree. Especially in this state. But Harrison couldn't bring himself to say the words, to take advantage of the situation.

"The only reason we're still here is because I was too afraid."

He squeezed her tighter, his gaze rising to the crooked balcony. It was so sad the only places she could find peace was on a busted old balcony and a big rock by the river. She deserved so much more.

Harrison dropped his cheek to her soft hair and thought about the buzzards in the kitchen. They didn't care about her. Whether she would be a distraction or not, she needed to be taken away from this place as much as Nathan.

He set her away from him and looked deep into her glorious, tear-filled eyes. "Juliet, I want you and Nathan to come home with me. For good."

SHE'D LOST HER MIND. That was the only explanation for what Juliet thought she'd heard Harrison say. She had to be hearing things, because no way would he have asked her to come home with him. No way at all.

Unless he'd said he wanted Nathan to come home with him, and her screwed-up mind had simply inserted the *you and* into his statement. Now that made sense.

Of course he'd want to take Nathan after what had happened. He was the guy who always did the right thing. But taking Nathan from her was *not* the right thing, no matter how bad she'd blown it.

She wiped the haze of tears from her eyes with her fingertips so he'd be sure to see her conviction when she met his gaze. "You can't have Nathan."

"Juliet, that's not what I…I want you *both* to come with me." He settled his hands on her shoulders. "This isn't about taking Nathan away from you. It's about getting you both away from here and into a life you deserve. A life where you can grow to reach your potential and be happy."

He waved a contemptuous hand up at the balcony. "And not just when you're sitting watching a river— and your life—pass you by. I know you're afraid of change, Juliet, but you're going to have to risk it for the sake of our child. And yourself."

At the mention of change and risk, Juliet's old defenses rose up around her like specters from a grave. "All while under your thumb," she retorted, and started to pull away. Her heart couldn't take this. Not today. He was offering her the sky, and she was afraid to fly.

Harrison made a rude noise and turned away from

her. "Juliet, please." He ran a hand through his hair. For the first time she noticed the rasp in his voice and the dark circles under his eyes. "Don't do this again. Not when there is so much at stake. If the Children's Services Department ever got a hold of this, things could easily get blown out of proportion and we'd have a hell of a mess on our hands."

Juliet's battered heart slammed to a halt. *The Children's Services Department?* She mouthed the words, unwilling to say them aloud for fear of producing a caseworker out of thin air. She wrapped her arms protectively around herself. "What do you mean?" she asked from low in her throat.

Harrison turned to look back at her. "Nothing." The worrisome expression on his face cleared. "Nothing we need to think about now."

Juliet felt her insides slowly turning to stone. *Please God, no,* she thought to herself. Harrison couldn't possibly be threatening her with Children's Services.

Could he?

Juliet felt an unholy calmness settle over her. He certainly had enough ammunition against her. Did he plan to use blackmail to get what he wanted?

Determined to find out what that was, she asked him flat out. "What is it that you want, Harrison?"

"I want to take you and Nathan away from here."

"To where?"

He reached out and wiped a stubborn tear from her cheek with the back of his index finger. "Home, with me."

Her heart started beating again, this time furiously. "To the Rivers estate in Plainview?"

"Yes. I want you and Nathan to move into the house."

Juliet brought her brows down, her pulse slowing. "Why?"

He ran his hand over his face in frustration. "I told you! I want you and Nathan to have better than this." He flung a sharp gesture at the store. Reaching for her again, he wrapped his warm hands around her upper arms and leaned down toward her face. "Come home with me, Juliet."

"Will you call the CSD on me if I don't?"

"No! That's not why I brought it up. I swear."

She searched his fierce gaze as best she could in the twilight, looking for his intent. She didn't know what to do. Her heart screamed for her to do as he asked. She felt so emotionally pummeled, so desperately in need of support and comfort, and the only person who could give her those things, besides Nathan, was standing right in front of her.

The tightness of her throat forced her to whisper. "Your father won't like it."

"To hell with my father. This is my decision. You and Nathan are a part of *my* life."

She squashed the thrill that rocketed through her. Part of his life or not, she would never be accepted in his world. "You shouldn't purposefully make him angry right now. What if he decides not to step aside and let you run the company?"

"He wouldn't do that. Not over me bringing you and Nathan home."

"But what if he does, Harrison? What if he denies you the one thing you've always wanted?"

"He won't."

For some reason his conviction rang hollow. "But

if he does, could you handle it? Would you still be happy with the risk you took?''

''You'll never get what you want in life if you don't take risks. My mother taught me that.''

''You said before, you loved her,'' she stated, thinking of her grandfather.

''Yes.''

''And she loved you?''

''She used to tell me so every day.'' His voice sounded small, almost faraway even though he stood not a foot from her.

She softened her tone. ''Don't you think she'd want you to be happy? Not to take a risk that could cost you the one thing you've always wanted?''

Harrison looked at her. The darkness kept her from discovering what might have been in his eyes.

Then her grandfather's favorite quote echoed in her head. Seeing its wisdom, she repeated it to Harrison.

''To thine own self be true, Harrison. To thine own self be true.'' Not expecting or wanting a response, Juliet turned and started toward the store.

''Juliet.''

Harrison's gentle call stopped her.

''Will you come home with me?''

She gave him her answer with the slightest movement of her head, then went inside. To pack her and Nathan's bags. Grandpa, God rest his soul, would understand if she didn't stay to run the store.

Because she was not a hypocrite.

WHILE JULIET wasn't a hypocrite, she certainly wasn't brave, so she sneaked upstairs, packed her and Nathan's things in her duffel, and tossed the army-green canvas bag down to Harrison from the wobbly

balcony. She wrapped Nathan and his bear in his crib
blanket without waking him and carried him downstairs as silently as she could. She couldn't face her
family and explain her actions right now. She just
couldn't.

How could she make them understand that to be
true to herself, she had to go with Harrison? She had
to take this chance.

Even though it scared the spit out of her.

But she wanted, more than anything, to be with
Harrison, so it was worth the risk. She hoped.

Seeming to read the terror on her face and understand, Harrison didn't say anything to her as she settled Nathan into his car seat. But when she moved to
go to the passenger side of the car, he stopped her
with a gentle hand to her cheek and brought her gaze
to his.

"It'll be okay," he whispered.

Juliet couldn't answer past the dread in her throat.

Harrison dipped his head and touched a light, sweet
kiss to her lips. It was the last thing she needed. Did
he plan to further close the distance between them?
Didn't he know a relationship between them would
never work?

Or would it? Could she find a way to bridge the
distance between their worlds? Convince him loving
wasn't so bad? Moving into the same house would be
a sure way to find out. She gave him a small smile.
His answering grin pumped strength into her weary
heart and wavering soul.

She felt much better as she slid into the smooth
leather interior of the car, but she still didn't want to
talk about what they were doing. If she talked, she

might find herself talking them both out of this insanity.

They drove to the Rivers estate in silence. But in a way the silence was worse. It allowed Harrison's presence to speak to her. She became aware of the warmth his big body radiated. The spiciness of his cologne mingled with the car's leather, creating a heady male scent. His wide, strong hands steered the sedan with ease and made her feel safe. There was so much about him that appealed to her. That she wanted.

Heaven help her.

Approaching the circular drive, she heard Harrison groan softly when a sleek, silver, Jaguar sports car, parked nearly in the center of the drive, appeared in his headlights.

"What?"

"My dad must have skipped the banquet after all."

This was going to be oh-so-much fun.

Harrison parked his car off to the side of the front door, and Juliet sat staring up at the beautiful house. A house full of Harrison's people.

She muttered, "I wish no one was home."

"We have to face them sometime, Juliet. It's better for everyone if we do it sooner rather than later."

She turned to look at him. "What are you going to say to them?"

Sliding his hands from the steering wheel, Harrison grabbed hold of one of her hands and gave it a squeeze. "That you and Nathan are moving in."

She couldn't bring herself to ask for how long. "Your dad will be thrilled."

He laughed. "Probably not. But Grandmother will

be. And I have a distinct feeling Ashley won't mind, either.''

Nathan woke up. At the sight of the huge house he yelled, ''Nanna!''

Harrison raised an amused-looking eyebrow at Juliet. ''Nanna?''

''She taught him to call her that.''

''Is that what he calls your mother?''

''No. My mom makes him call her Phyllis, but since he can't say that, he mostly grunts at her.''

Harrison regarded her silently, his pity sneaking out through the softness of his eyes. The reminder of the world she was leaving gave her the kick in the butt she needed to get out of the car and on with a better life for her child.

''If you'll get my duffel, I'll get Nathan.''

Harrison's eyes cleared and he grinned. ''Deal.''

He didn't seem to be having second thoughts.

Yet.

The butler opened the heavy, carved door before they reached the top step. ''Good evening, Mr. Rivers, Miss Jones.'' He reached out a finger and touched a groggy Nathan, who was balanced on Juliet's hip, lightly on the nose. ''And Master Nathan. It's so good to see you are no worse for wear.''

Juliet wasn't surprised to discover Dorothy Rivers didn't exclude her staff from family worries. Of course, how could a person work in someone else's home and not know everything that went on? Donavon probably knew every juicy little bit.

She shifted from one sandaled foot to the other. God only knew what he'd heard about her.

To Juliet and Harrison he said, ''It's truly a blessing,'' as he ushered them in.

"That's the understatement of the millennium, Donavon," Harrison answered, then smiled down at Juliet. His repeating her phrase sent rejuvenating warmth into her parts frozen by dread. She returned his smile even though hers felt a little weak at the corners.

Harrison handed her bag over to Donavon. "Could you put this in the yellow guest room?"

Without so much as a blink Donavon answered, "Most certainly," and took the faded old army duffel, carrying it off like one of Dorothy's best.

With a big hand to the small of Juliet's back, Harrison urged her toward a set of double doors. She tucked Nathan's head beneath her chin and hesitated at the sound of muffled voices behind the doors.

"Come, it's off to the lion's den," he said.

"Why do I get the feeling you're not joking?" she croaked.

He flashed her a wry smile, but continued to guide her toward her doom. When she halted, he glanced down at her feet as if he thought her sandals had glue on them. "Come on. Let's get this done." He looked back into her eyes and added, "Grandmother won't rest until she sees for herself that Nathan is all right."

Juliet scowled at him. Reminding her of her failings as a mother was not what she needed right now. She dug in her heels further.

With a sigh, Harrison went forward without her and pulled open the study doors. The flee instinct had Juliet stepping into the shadow of one of the doors.

"Harrison," she heard Dorothy exclaim. Nathan came fully awake and struggled to get down. Juliet whispered, "Not yet, sweetie," then shifted him to her other hip and edged closer to the door, but not so close that she couldn't see into the study.

She was such a coward.

Dorothy rose from a chair in front of the cold fireplace and went to her grandson. "I've been very concerned. Tell me, darling, what has happened?"

Harrison took his grandmother's hands in his. "What should have happened some time ago." He turned toward the doorway, obviously where he expected her and Nathan to be standing.

She knew he wanted her to join him, but she couldn't. Not yet.

His handsome brow crinkled in a puzzled frown and he looked about to call to her when his father, looking like a refugee from *Dynasty* in his tuxedo, stepped around the desk and interrupted him.

"Glad to hear you've come to your senses, son. I'm assuming we're going to sue for *complete* custody?"

Juliet felt the bile kick up in her stomach.

Harrison shot his father a hard look. "I'm not suing anyone for anything, but Nathan *is* coming to live here."

George rocked back on his heels. "Excellent. Now, I've already taken the liberty of contacting some of the better boarding schools. They aren't as easy to come by anymore around here. And they have waiting lists…" He trailed off when he noticed Harrison's glare. "You take issue with my involvement?"

Juliet hugged Nathan tightly to her. *Boarding schools, my rear.* She would disappear with Nathan before she let them ship him off. The urge to leave right then and there made the bottoms of her feet itch.

What had she been thinking coming here? What was Harrison thinking?

In answer to her question he said, "There will be no boarding schools and no custody battles. Juliet and I have agreed to—"

George butted in. "I'm glad she came to her senses. I'm sure she realized after being here today that this is where Nathan belongs. Though I still think your only course is to cut ties with that bunch of inbred yahoos by gaining complete custody."

Dorothy drew in a sharp breath. "Now, George—"

"No." His father held up his hand to stave off Dorothy's protest. "No, Mother. You have to admit that Harrison's son is in peril with his mother. If not physical peril anymore—one could only hope she'd learn from this latest incident—then most certainly psychological peril. The girl is what she is. What her environment has made her. And, Harrison, if you allow your son to remain in that environment in any way, shape or form, or to even have much in the way of contact with his mother, he'll be tainted in the same manner. Branded with the same epithet."

Juliet held her heart still in her chest, waiting for the pronouncement of the verdict she'd been handed at her birth. The words reverberated in her head even before they left George Rivers's mouth.

"White trash."

Juliet blinked away her tears, blaming them on outrage, not the hurt that made her feel like she was being filleted. A hurt she couldn't bear to acknowledge. Besides, she didn't care what that jerk thought of her. Other than Nathan, the only person's opinion that mattered was the big, glorious man standing in the center of the room, still gently cradling his grand-mother's frail hands in his own.

"Dad," Harrison said in a tone as smooth and hard as steel. "Juliet has more dedication to those she loves in her little finger than you have in your entire uptight body. *She* would never refuse to see someone she loved just because it caused her pain. If you want to see or speak to me again, you'd better rethink your opinion of the mother of my child." He sounded sin-cere, but had he said it because he knew the object of this nightmare conversation stood outside the door? Or because he wanted to punish his father for not being there when his mother died?

A thought bloomed in Juliet's head and spread down to her belly like a strangling weed. He'd already told her he thought it was a bad idea to care very much. What if his father eventually struck a cord in Harrison that changed his mind about her?

The man was right after all. A bitter taste filled her mouth. No matter how long she had fought to deny it, to refuse it, the fact remained—she and her family were losers. Dead-enders.

Trash.

She didn't belong in this wonderful house with its lovely paintings, side tables and level porches. She didn't belong with that incredible man, no matter how right being in his arms felt.

Hiking her sweet, once-again-sleepy baby higher on her hip, she started backing away from the door. She was totally delusional to have even considered coming home with Harrison, let alone actually doing it. The smart thing would be to get out of there before she made a bigger fool of herself. But she needed their stuff.

Juliet turned and headed for the stairs. The Yellow Room. She had to find the Yellow Room. Harrison had told Donavon to stick her duffel in the Yellow Room. How could she have thought she'd belong in a place with named rooms?

Pausing at the base of the huge, free-standing curving staircase, she tried to remember which way Donavon had gone, but she hadn't paid attention. And the tears in her eyes made it hard to see. This house was so damn big she didn't stand a chance of finding her and Nathan's things before Harrison came looking for her. She didn't want to face him with the truth about her ringing in her ears. She turned on her heel and headed for the front door. He could mail her the stupid duffel.

Hearing footsteps coming fast on the marble-tile floor behind her, Juliet increased her pace. Wouldn't it be rich to have the butler rush to open the door for her and usher her, bawling, out into the night. She yanked the door open herself with her free hand and hurried outside, not bothering to close it behind her.

"Juliet!" Harrison. It was Harrison behind her.

Her heart, what was left of it, caved in on itself like a stomped-on can at the sound of the emotion in his voice. How could she tell him goodbye?

Chapter Eleven

"Juliet, wait!" Harrison shouted more forcefully at her back. When he'd first seen her heading for the door he'd ridiculously thought she might be going out to retrieve something from his car. But when she ran across the drive and headed for the lawn in the direction of the main road he knew she was bolting. Her pace wasn't that of someone going for an evening stroll.

He wasn't surprised. Damn it. Why hadn't he cut his father off sooner? Before his dad spewed out all those awful, hurtful things about her? She would never gain confidence in herself with his father adding to the damage already done to her. Her running away wouldn't help, either. And, what was most important, he wasn't about to let her disappear from his life.

He broke into a run and reached for Juliet's elbow. "Juliet." He snagged her arm and brought her up short. "Where do you think you're going?" he asked in a low voice, mindful of his sleepy son on her hip.

She wouldn't look at him. "Where I belong." She snatched her arm out of his grasp.

Harrison damned himself for not sending her and

Nathan straight upstairs before he went to talk to his
father. "You belong here."

"Right." She curled her lip, but its trembling de-
feated her sneer. "I'm not welcome in there—"

He took hold of her arm again. "Listen, I told
him—"

"No. You listen, Harrison. I'm not welcome in
there. And for good reason. I don't belong in there,
or anywhere else in your world. I don't know how to
dress, how to act. I'm no debutante. I could never
belong with you." Her last word caught on a sob.

"You're wrong, Juliet. You belong where you'll
be appreciated. And that's with me, in there."

She shook her head sadly, as if she pitied him. "It
showed in how your father is just dying to throw his
arms around me and welcome me to the club. I'm
certain he can't wait to split the morning paper with
me over a cup of joe—sorry, I mean a double latte,
skinny. No, wait—" she held up her hand, looking a
little wild around the eyes "—you guys probably
have Donavon read the paper for you."

"Are you done?"

"Yes, I'm done." She pulled her arm out of his
hand again. "I am absolutely done." She hitched Nathan higher on her hip and started to walk away.

"Like hell," he growled. "I'm not going to let you
walk away from me."

She stopped cold and turned to face him. "Why,
Harrison? Why? Because you can't stand it when
things don't go the way you want? Because you can't
stand not being in control?"

He stared at her, beautiful in the moonlight and her
anger. Why, indeed? Why was her walking away
from him tonight absolutely, positively unacceptable?

He didn't fear losing contact with Nathan; he believed her when she'd said she wouldn't keep Nathan from him. No matter where she ended up, he felt certain he would still have access to his son.

So why was he so against her living somewhere other than the estate? It wasn't as if having her close was the answer to his problems. Far from it. Because he *did* like being in control, and she threatened his ability to maintain control with every breath she took.

He simply refused to lose her. And he wanted more than anything to take care of her.

Guilt didn't seem the likely motivator anymore; there were far too many different ways he could have assuaged his remorse for altering the course of her life. If she were right and he did have some unconscious need to try to run her life, then so be it, because he was past trying to fight the protective urges she stirred in him, and he profoundly believed she would benefit from them.

He extended a hand toward her. "I don't want to control you in the way you think, Juliet. This isn't some power trip. I want to help you. Make your life better."

She didn't take his hand.

He blew out a breath and looked up at the star-filled sky. The only thing she'd believe was the truth, even if he wasn't prepared to explain the reasons behind it to her or himself. "I want to take care of you. You and Nathan." He looked back at her, wishing he could see what judgment her expression held. "Let me take care of you."

She relaxed her rigid posture and retraced the steps separating them. "Oh, Harrison, we just can't—"

The sound of his grandmother's voice cut her off.

"Excuse me, you two," she called to them as she crossed the drive, loud enough to get their attention but not loud enough to rouse Nathan.

Harrison stood silent until she reached them, his emotions running too high to trust his voice.

"It's getting a bit chilly out here for our little angel. I would have fetched him sooner, but I only just learned from Donavon that Harrison had brought the two of you home with him. I'll take Nathan inside and get him tucked in bed." She reached for him, ignoring Juliet's half step away, and took the quilt-wrapped toddler.

Juliet looked lost and alone without her baby in her arms.

His grandmother sent her a reassuring smile. "The Yellow Room has a queen-size bed, so there will be plenty of space for you to cuddle in with him when you two are done out here." She turned and started walking back to the house. Over her shoulder she said, "As soon as he's comfortable here, we'll get him set up in a room of his own with a crib and everything."

Grandmother stopped and looked back at them. "Oh, and Juliet. I am so thrilled to have you moving in, also. Don't you worry about Harrison's father. He'll change his tune the second he gets to know you. And if he doesn't, you go right ahead and give him the toe of your shoe like Harrison did. While change can at times be frightening, it is the only way to discover new possibilities." Dorothy Rivers's grin outshone the moon.

God, how he loved that old lady.

Harrison pulled in a deep, calming breath of crisp night air. Crossing his arms over his chest, he turned away from his grandmother's retreating back and faced Juliet with both brows raised. "See? I'm not the only one who thinks change is good. Do you believe *her?*"

Juliet brought her big, tear-filled gaze up to his, her lower lip trembling. "Are you sure this will be okay? With everybody?"

"I'm certain."

She visibly swallowed. "But your dad could get even by deciding not to retire or he could pick someone else to be chairman."

He took her hands in his. They were icy-cold. "Sweetheart, let me worry about the company. I'm good at it. Now, let's get you inside."

Juliet allowed him to walk her back to the house, her slender hand cold and stiff in his. When he continued walking past the study where his father was pacing back and forth, the look she gave his dad changed from wary to speculative.

She continued to watch the study doors as Harrison led her upstairs. "Harrison?" she asked softly.

"What?"

"Has your dad always been that..."

"Judgmental?" he offered.

"Big of a jerk?"

He chuckled, delighting in her straightforwardness. He didn't get enough of that in his world. "No. Actually, he was a pretty nice guy, and a great businessman, before my mom died."

She nodded. "Maybe you should send him to count gold Formica speckles with good old Ophelia."

Harrison nearly stumbled at Juliet's quick take on his father. "I'm not sure I could do that to your mother."

She made a noise in her throat. "Mom probably would be a good match for him." She shook her head. "It's wild how different people deal with death in so many different ways."

Ignoring the familiar twinge of pain in his heart, Harrison guided her toward the west wing, previously occupied only by his grandmother. "That's what happens when you care too much."

Her grip on his hand tightened ever so slightly. "Too bad we can't control how much we care."

"Who says we can't?"

She gave a mirthless laugh. "You're kidding yourself."

He was saved from having to argue the point when they reached the Yellow Room and heard Grandmother singing a lullaby. They stepped into the dimly lit suite as Grandmother rose from the bed. Nathan was snuggled down and clearly asleep.

"Ah, good," she whispered. "I didn't want to leave him alone in a strange room until you returned, but I'm afraid if I stayed next to him on the bed I'd be asleep in a moment or two, also, so I was moving to the chair. But since you're here, Juliet, I'll put myself to bed. See you in the morning, darlings." She patted Harrison on the arm as she walked past.

With raised brows, Juliet took in the pleasant-sized room and adjoining bathroom decorated entirely in pale-yellow tones.

He had to chuckle. "Yep. It's yellow."

"I pretty much figured it would be," she whispered back, and slipped her hand from his to go to the bed. She lightly touched Nathan's head. "I'm glad he's asleep. He's had a heck of a day."

Thinking of the turmoil they'd all been through since that afternoon, Harrison said, ''We all have.''

Juliet nodded silently.

Though he trusted the doctor's prognosis that Nathan was fine, he offered, ''Do you want me to set my alarm and come wake him in a few hours, like the doctor recommended?''

She shook her head. ''No, I'll do it. But, thanks.''

He nodded. ''Then I'll let you get to sleep. If you need anything, Grandmother's room is at the end of this hall.''

''And your room?''

His heart picked up its tempo at her soft question. All sorts of erotic possibilities raced through his mind, but he shut them down as quickly as he could while clearing his throat. She was undoubtedly only curious. ''Down the opposite hall, around the corner, second door on the left.''

She nodded again. Harrison hesitated at the door, thinking she might say something more. When she remained silent, he forced himself to leave. The possibility of late-night visits to each other's room was *not* why he'd brought her here.

''Good night,'' he said just before he closed the door behind him.

An incredible feeling of satisfaction seeped through him as he headed for his room. His son was in a safe, stable environment with both parents, Dad would hand over the chairmanship of the company at his retirement party, and Juliet was close enough at hand that he wouldn't have to spend all his time thinking about her.

His world was well on its way to being exactly how he wanted it. Assuming, of course, he'd be able to sleep knowing his favorite fantasy was only half a house away.

JULIET WOKE to the sound of breaking glass.

The second the pale-yellow walls, crown molding and the empty pillow next to her came into focus, she jerked upright, rigid with dread.

Expensive glass.

She quickly scanned the room for her toddler and any sign of destruction, but when she spotted the open door, she threw back the covers and bolted from the bed, not caring that she only had on an oversize football jersey. Nathan was on the loose in the mansion. A mansion filled with pricey breakables.

She tore into the hallway and spotted Nathan standing at the top of the staircase, his little hands curled into fists and tucked beneath his chin in his *oops* pose, looking down the stairs. Good Lord, he'd undoubtedly pitched something down the staircase. At least he hadn't joined whatever it was for the ride.

Juliet pulled in a steadying breath and made her way as calmly as she could toward her son. "Nathan, baby, what'cha doing out of Momma's bed?"

Nathan gave a guilty start. Fortunately she was close enough to him by then to put her hands on him and pull him away from the top stair. Though he'd become a master at sliding down the narrow staircase at home—make that their old home—she wasn't sure if he'd be as cautious with the Rivers's wide-open, curving staircase. Not to mention that the fall he took yesterday might have affected his balance.

With an impressive show of bravado, he smiled his *ain't I a stinker* smile, then glanced from her to the stairs. "Dada play," he offered, obviously trying to put a positive spin on his destruction.

Juliet followed Nathan's gaze, and sure enough, there was Harrison, in shorts and a tank top, frozen in the act of starting up the stairs with his fisted hands full of something.

He blew out a breath. "Oh, good. You can keep a hold of him. I had him sitting on the stairs down here, but in the time it took me to pick up these," he opened his fists and showed her the chunks of clear crystal, "the little scamp had climbed all the way up."

Dreading what the pieces of crystal had once been in the shape of, she asked, "What broke?"

He shrugged as if it didn't matter and stepped back down on the foyer's black and white marble tiles. "An ornamental ball." Kneeling carefully, he started picking up more of the crystal.

Though she knew it was a silly question, she asked anyway, "Did Nathan do it?"

He sent her a lopsided, guilty grin that echoed Nathan's so much her heart swelled until her chest hurt. "I guess it wasn't such a good idea to let him hold the ball while I carried him down the stairs."

Juliet pulled in a deep breath to crowd her stupid heart back into its dark corner and chided, "Not when the ball is glass!" She'd be in big trouble if she had to parent him, too. Hadn't she proved yesterday how dicey her abilities were?

Not sure at what point on the trip down the glass ball had been launched, she returned her attention to Nathan and said, "Sit right here for Momma, sugar, and stay put, please." She settled him on his bottom away from the stairs but close enough to still see his father. When she was certain he'd heard, she hurried down the stairs, the plush, cream-colored runner cushioning her bare feet and her football jersey nightshirt flapping around her thighs.

Harrison sat back on his heels and watched her with a dorky, slack-jawed kind of look on his face until she was almost to the bottom step. Jeez, didn't he care that an undoubtedly expensive ball-thing had been busted to smithereens?

He finally seemed to snap-to and raised a hand to ward her off. "Stop. Stay on the stairs. Your feet are bare."

"I know that." An old pro at cleaning up Nathan's *oopses,* she ignored his warning and stepped carefully onto the tile, avoiding the glass he had yet to pick up.

"Juliet, you'll cut your feet. I can get this."

"No. Nathan is my responsibility." And she'd be damned if she'd draw her suitability for the job into question anymore. After a quick glance to make sure their baby was still sitting back from the stairs, she squatted next to Harrison and started picking up the pieces. Fortunately, the crystal had been thick and broke into large chunks. Unfortunately, that was probably a sign of high quality. The thought made her hand start to shake. It would take her forever to replace the thing. "I'll clean up after him."

Harrison reached out and covered her hand, stilling it. The warmth of his touch warmed her clear to the soles of her bare feet.

"Juliet." The way his deep, smooth voice said her name gave her more bittersweet pleasure than the most fattening Valentine chocolate. "It was really my fault."

The same guilt that had tore at her yesterday made

her unable to meet his gaze. "But he was sleeping with me. I should have woken up when he got out of bed."

"I got him out of bed."

She quickly looked at him and searched his deep-river eyes for an explanation. If she didn't know better, she would have sworn a blush spread under his tan.

"It was nearly nine, which, I'm sure, is considered nearly afternoon for a toddler, so I thought I'd peek in and check on you two before I went to the weight room."

His attire finally registered in her brain, and she allowed her gaze a quick trip over what could only be described as a beefcake buffet. He might as well have been bare-chested for the way his gray weight-lifting-style tank top covered his muscle-capped shoulders and mounded pecs. And while his black shorts were probably long and loose when he stood, in his current crouch, they'd pulled high and tight to expose enough powerful, perfectly hairy leg to make her mouth go dry.

He continued with his explanation and she had to jerk her gaze back to his. "Nathan was still lying next to you, but he was wide awake. I knew it would only be a matter of time before he woke you up, too, and since you needed the sleep, I slipped in and picked him up." He shrugged a thick shoulder. "Couldn't help it. He was grinning at me...and well, you know."

"Yes, I know," she croaked. Like she knew what she wanted to do to Harrison's magnificent body. Clearing her throat, she added, "He's irresistible."

Just like his daddy. Slipping her hand from beneath

his before the contact and his masculine seductiveness made her say something that might jeopardize whatever it was building between them, she focused on the broken crystal. "But you should try to resist letting him hold pricey breakables. Especially when they are in the shape of balls, which he thinks are meant to be chucked."

He laughed. The sound warmed her to her soul. "You have the best way of putting things. You're right, I should have resisted that particular urge."

The image of other urges he hadn't resisted brought her gaze back to his. The warmth she'd been feeling grew until she realized the sensation hadn't come entirely from his laugh or his touch. And it didn't all stem from the shadows of shared passions swimming in his dark-green eyes, either.

"Oh, my gosh!" Juliet flattened her palm against the tile floor. The heat radiating from it was unmistakable.

Harrison's dark-blond brows slammed together. "What? Did you cut yourself? Are you all right?"

She couldn't help giggling in delight over his obvious concern. No one had been that concerned about her. Ever. "No, no. The tile. It's heated!"

His eyelids slid closed, and he let out a noisy breath. "Oh. Yes, it is. Grandmother had heating coils laid under them when the floors were redone after the '96 flood."

"Wow." She stood up to more fully absorb the heat through the bottoms of her feet. "This is so awesome."

He shook his head in a bemused way. "I guess I've grown so used to it that I don't notice it anymore." Raising a brow in a sinfully sensuous way, he gave her his lopsided grin. "I could have used it as a selling point to get my barefoot girl here sooner."

Unsure whether to be angry that he thought her so easily manipulated, flattered because he'd wanted her living with him sooner or hot and bothered by his suggestiveness—heck, by his mere presence—Juliet latched on to the first part of his comment instead. "So you don't get any kind of pleasure from this sort of luxury?"

He shrugged again. "There's pleasure," he paused, and sent her a look that should have set off the smoke alarms, "And then there's *pleasure*."

Suddenly very aware that she wore nothing more than an oversize football jersey her body wanted *off*, she dropped back down and snatched up more chunks of crystal. "Is there a garbage can handy? We really should finish cleaning up this glass."

As if on cue, Donavon appeared from a room off the foyer with a broom and dustpan. "Allow me," he said genially.

Both Juliet and Harrison stood and carefully dumped their handfuls of glass in the dustpan. Before she knew what he intended, Harrison whisked her into his arms and started carrying her up the stairs.

Frantically tugging at the hem of her jersey to make sure she wasn't flashing Donavon with her Sunday undies, she squawked, "What are you doing?"

"I don't want you cutting those feet of yours. Nor do I want you worrying about Nathan instead of getting the rest you need. I have something to show you."

By the time they reached the top of the stairs, Nathan was jumping up and down and gleefully shrieking, "Mamma up! Mamma up!"

Dizzy from his actions and desperate to keep the chaos to a minimum, Juliet pleaded, "Put me down."

"But of course, m'lady." Harrison released his hold on the back of her legs and set her lightly on her feet without the slightest effort.

Her heart beat wildly from being in his arms. "What did you want to show me?" she asked in an embarrassingly breathy voice.

He swept up their baby the same way he had her and said, "Nathan's room," then strode down the hall.

He stopped in front of the door directly across from her yellow room and Juliet hurried to catch up with him. Shifting Nathan to one arm, he opened the door with a flourish.

Expecting a guest room much like her own, though ridiculously curious about its color, she peeked in, then blinked. The room looked like the inside of a Toys-N-Stuff van. She sucked in a breath. The very Toys-N-Stuff van she'd sent packing. The only new additions were an unassembled, elaborate white crib and a matching armoire.

From beside her Harrison said, "Some assembly required, of course."

Distrust oozed through the cracks made by her insecurities and threatened to smother the pleasures of only a moment ago. "You'd planned on him moving here all along?"

"You and him."

His look of patient tenderness sealed up the cracks quite nicely. Maybe this is what he'd meant when he'd said he wanted to take care of her. Overwhelmed, Juliet stared at the room filled with everything an eighteen-month-old boy could want, and all she could think was that she and Nathan had moved into Harrison Rivers's house and their lives would never be the same again. But would Nathan grow up like his father and not even notice how lucky he was?

Not if she could help it. And maybe Harrison would end up better for it, too.

LATE THAT NIGHT, despite having spent her first day at "Richville" herding her curious toddler away from huge but still-tippy floor vases and table runners loaded with a million breakables just itching to be yanked off, Juliet couldn't sleep. She needed to think, to assure herself she'd made the right decision moving here, and the only place she could do that was down by the river.

She glanced at the video monitor glowing on her nightstand. Nathan slept so soundly in his newly assembled crib across the hall that she wasn't worried about him waking, but she waited until after midnight before she slipped into her jeans and a T-shirt and ventured from her room. She didn't want to risk running into George Rivers on her way out.

She'd successfully avoided him during the day, and she wanted to keep it that way. The man's opinion of her wasn't going to change, regardless of what Harrison or Dorothy thought, and Juliet would just as soon dodge him as much as possible until she decided what to do.

She hadn't been so successful avoiding the father of her child. He had decided to forgo his workout in favor of playing with Nathan while she showered and dressed. Unfortunately, he hadn't felt it necessary to change out of his skimpy, disastrously appealing exercise clothes the entire day.

He had to know what he was doing to her, so why the torture? He'd gotten his way, hadn't he? Maybe it was his way of getting back at her for messing up his orderly, controlled life by getting pregnant.

He hadn't acted particularly vengeful during the day, though. He'd seemed really happy to have them there, even going out to pick up fast-food hamburgers and eating them with her and Nat in the kitchen because that's what their son had wanted.

She didn't know what to think as she made her way downstairs and to the back of the house, thankfully without smacking into anything. Momentarily daunted by the security system, she figured out which button to push on the small control panel next to the French doors to allow her to slip outside without alerting the marines. The bright, silvered light of a nearly full moon lit the way out onto the veranda and down to the sprawling lawn. The perfectly tended grass felt like cool, slightly moist shag carpeting beneath her bare feet.

She retraced the path Harrison had taken her on yesterday—seemingly ages ago—until she reached the low dock extending out into the inky blackness of the river. Though the Rivers estate sat on a much more refined section of the Mac, the moist air smelled the same, and she pulled in a soothing lungful as she walked toward the lone chair standing guard at the end of the dock. She could think here, maybe even better than on her stupid old balcony.

Grinding her teeth at the pang of loss the thought of the balcony sent through her, she had nearly reached the large wooden chair before she realized with a start that it was occupied by a very large body in a dark shirt and chinos.

"Couldn't sleep?" Harrison's silky-smooth voice touched her as effectively as his hand and sent her blood pounding through her body.

"No," she practically croaked. She should have known she would never be able to escape this man long enough to think straight for five seconds, let alone sleep. This was his home, for heaven's sake, and whether she ran into him like this or not, he would be everywhere, always. And she couldn't imagine a sweeter torture.

The chair groaned as he pushed himself to his feet. "Me, neither."

She would have backed away from him, but she wasn't sure where the dock ended behind her and she couldn't manage to look away from his moonshine-handsomeness long enough to check. He towered above her and crowded into her personal space without even trying, unwittingly reminding her of the glorious knight who used to sweep into her dreams and effortlessly fill all the aching empty places in her body and soul.

Would he ever want to play that role again? Did she dare ask him?

He pointed a hand toward the chair. "Have a seat."

She couldn't have moved if her butt were on fire.

So it was understandable that she didn't flinch when he raised a hand and swept a strand of her hair back from her face and tucked it behind her ear. The now familiar gesture made her heart ache.

"I know it's not the same as your balcony, sweetheart, but I think you'll be able to find the same sort of peace here as you did there." His voice caressed her again and made her sway toward him.

Didn't he know the only place she felt at peace was in his arms?

He flattened his palm against her cheek and ran the warm pad of his thumb over her lips. "I just wish you'd trust me again, Juliet. Like you did that day two years ago."

Closing her eyes against his agonizing tenderness, she whispered, "It's me I don't trust."

"I know exactly what you mean," he answered, and pulled her toward him, his mouth finding hers without hesitation.

She returned his kiss with the same conviction because deep down, in the place where her dreams hid out and refused to die, she did trust him, with all her heart.

Just as she loved him.

She slipped her arms around his neck, and he gathered her against his big body, his kiss growing almost frantic. She took everything he gave and still wanted more.

Instead of holding her tighter, touching her more, he loosened his hold and brought his hands up to capture her face. He pulled his mouth from hers.

"Juliet," he gasped. "I need you so much. Let me make love to you again. Let me be inside of you."

Before she could answer, he kissed her again and grazed a hot hand over the thin T-shirt material covering her breast, as if he thought she needed further proof of his passion for her, then he gathered her to him and hugged her tight.

Into her hair he murmured, "And this time it won't cost you so much. I have protection. You'll never have to pay for my irresponsibility again."

Juliet choked out a laugh. He had to be kidding.

Protection or not, loving Harrison would cost her, every single day of her life. "Were you expecting to bump into me tonight? Or do you just stuff a condom in your pocket every morning along with your keys?"

He made a noise in the back of his throat and squeezed her tighter. "I probably should. You make me nuts." He ran a hand up her back and into her hair and coaxed her head back so she would look at him.

While the light of the moon undoubtedly showed him all the bittersweet vulnerability she felt, the emotions fueling his passion remained shadowed from her. Would she ever really know why he wanted her? Did he even know? Not that it mattered. She couldn't control herself any better than he could.

He kissed her lightly, sucking her lower lip gently between his, then whispered, "But I had hoped you would need to come down to the river as much as I did. It seems to be the one place where things are clear." He kissed her again. "I can't deny it anymore, Juliet. I want to make love to you again."

On the verge of tears from her weakness for him but wanting him all the same, Juliet turned her head and nodded toward a cluster of young birch trees growing at the edge of the river, down from the dock. They created a tiny grotto. "There. Over there."

With the strength of a man who'd stepped beyond his restraint, Harrison hoisted her off her feet, gripped her bottom with both hands so she had to wrap her legs around his waist, and carried her off the dock to the trees without a single misstep. He dropped to one knee and laid her back on the sheltered patch of tended lawn. The sharp scent of crushed grass rose around them and added a natural blessing to the moment.

Staring down at her with pupils blown wide with desire, he whispered huskily, "You are so beautiful, Juliet. So beautiful and special."

He loomed large above her, masculine and protective, and his sweet words opened her like a key. She reached for him, pulling his mouth to hers. With her tongue touching his, she kissed him for all she was worth, letting loose all the longing and need that had weighted her down for so long. Only Harrison's big body settling onto hers kept her from joining the stars, just as he had when their passion had exploded the last time by the river.

There was so much of him, all hard and strong and hot, and she wanted to touch every inch of him, to convey through her fingertips what her heart was screaming—*You're the only man I'll ever love.* Gripping the back of his shirt in her fists, she pulled it over his head like a dirty fighter in a brawl.

He helped her by yanking the shirt the rest of the way off, then touched her in return, slipping his hands beneath her T-shirt and worshipping her bare flesh. "You set me on fire, Juliet," he groaned, and pushed her shirt up and off.

"Then get ready to burn," she vowed, and ran her hand down his hard chest, following the path of fine hair to his waistband. She unfastened his pants, pushed them out of the way, and made him suck in a breath when she told him with her hand what she wanted him to do to her, how she wanted him to do it.

Juliet wanted, needed, Harrison to make love to her slowly and gently and wonderfully, too. Just as he had before.

And he did.

In the moon-dappled beauty of the secluded haven, Harrison tucked his shirt beneath her, slid her jeans from her legs, trailing delicious kisses in their wake, then donned his protection and settled his big, hot body on top of hers. The heat of his chest was like a warm, moist kiss on her breasts compared to the crispness of the night air. Sliding his strong arms beneath her, he slid himself inside her and made love to her exactly how she wanted him to. Only he added a heartbreaking tenderness that had tears slipping from the corners of her eyes as he moved his hard length in and out of her.

She loved him for it. She loved him for every whispered word of praise, every reverent touch, every fiery kiss. He was always so strong and sure of himself, but when he held her in his arms, he made her feel that she had the power, that she had worth.

Desperate to show him he was the only man she would ever feel this way about, the only man she would ever love, Juliet grabbed fistfuls of hair on both sides of his head and pulled his mouth from hers.

''Look at me,'' she said between panting breaths that blended with the sounds of the river and the trees. Finding his soul in the shadows of his eyes, she hooked her bare heels behind his muscular thighs just above his pushed-down chinos and increased the tempo until their worlds shattered in exquisite, blinding shudders.

He captured her cry of pleasure with his mouth and mingled it with his own.

In that splintered, incredible moment in time, Juliet accepted, just as she had over two years ago, that she would never be the same again.

Chapter Twelve

They walked back to the moon-washed mansion together, their spent passion a physical thing between them that Juliet couldn't ignore. While Harrison didn't seem to regret making love with her—he'd kissed her sweetly, tenderly before he leveraged himself off her and helped her don her jeans and picked grass from her hair with a chuckle or two—she needed to hear him say the words.

Swinging her arms back and forth to pretend a casualness she didn't feel, she took the leap. "So," she offered softly, "is this going to be a 'meet me at the dock at midnight' kind of thing? Because I'm not sure how game I'm going to be, come later this fall. It's nippy enough as it is."

He glanced at her, studying her with his boardroom face. "So you're okay with this?"

She wrapped her arms around her middle. "That depends on what *this* is."

He made a noise. "I know what you mean."

Oh, now that was vague. Juliet squeezed her arms tighter around her. Did she dare go down this road right now, with her body still warmed by his touch and her mouth tender from his kisses? But she might not get another chance to find out what moved her tarnished knight to take her in his arms.

''The thing is, Harrison, I'm over here thinking, 'what's going to happen to me if he gets tired of me, or comes to his senses, or decides to listen to his father after all?' I'm just not sure I can sit around the *mansion* waiting for any or all of those things to happen, hoping to be with you as much as I can until I have to leave.''

He stopped and studied her some more in the moonlight. She was about to tell him to forget she'd opened her big mouth when he said, ''You won't ever have to leave, Juliet.''

Praying for some sort of declaration of feelings toward her, she braved a ''Why?''

He peeled one of her hands from her side and gripped it in his big, warm one. ''Nathan, for starters.''

Hope trickled away like water in the gutter. She pressed, ''I know you care about him, Harrison, but do you love him?''

''Yes. I do,'' he answered in a voice so low it rumbled.

''How much?''

He pulled in a shaky breath that tore at her heart. ''More than I thought possible.''

''Too much?''

His full brows came together. ''What do you mean?''

''When we first really talked down by my stretch of the river, you said that it's never good to love someone too much.''

His frown deepened. ''I was talking about something different. Loving a child is different.''

Dreading what he might say but needing to hear the truth, she asked, "Different from what?"

He looked at her like a doctor about to tell a patient she had terminal cancer. "Different from how a man loves a woman. Like how my dad loved my mother. Giving up yourself like that—making someone else the best part of you is...well, it's stupid. Because if they die or leave, or whatever, what's left of you is useless and bitter."

She sucked in a breath. How could he say such a thing right after touching her soul from the inside? Clearly her love for Harrison would never be returned. Fighting the tears burning in the back of her throat, she argued, "But Nathan *is* the best part of me."

He took her other hand in his. "The difference is that with a child, you don't have a choice. I had no choice in loving Nathan too much." His voice caught. "He's my son."

Though the shards of her heart felt like they were digging into her chest, she forced a smile. "And I'm his mother."

He pulled her hands toward him, forcing her to take the step that separated them. "You are so much more than that, sweetheart."

He dropped a sweet kiss on her lips that couldn't be mistaken for anything but a peace offering to a lover, before releasing one of her hands and heading them toward the house.

Okay, so she would never be the love of his life. At least she was *in* his life. She couldn't help tightening her hold on his hand as they climbed the stairs to the veranda. He responded with a slight squeeze of his own.

Maybe she should fight for his love. Show him that she could be what he needed in the light of day as well as the dead of night, that giving himself up to her wouldn't cost him. Convince him that loving someone so much you lose control was a good thing.

She'd already taken the biggest chance of her life by moving here with him. What more would she be risking by trying to get him to love her, to make a real family with her and Nathan?

Her pride, that's all.

As he opened the French doors and released her hand to step inside and enter a code into the security system panel, she looked back at the beauty of the night and decided it would be a price worth paying.

She loved him with every inch of her being. If that wasn't enough to bridge the gap between their worlds, what else could? There had to be a way to keep his loving her from hurting his chances of fulfilling his dreams. There *had* to be a way to do that.

Harrison recaptured her hand and started them down the hall to the front staircase, but Juliet pulled away from him. Protecting his chances had better start now. Being caught strolling hand in hand with him after midnight would not help him snag the top spot in his old man's company. As loud as she dared, she whispered, "We really shouldn't go waltzing upstairs together. Why don't you go raid the fridge, or something, while I head up."

With a sexy, butter-melting smile, he said, "To my room, right? While I don't mind sheds cars or riverbanks, I do want to get you into my bed sometime."

Though the prospect made all sorts of muscles clench with want when she would have sworn they'd be satisfied for a week, she shook her head. "We can't. It's not like you live alone. I couldn't bear getting caught.''

He considered her for a moment, then ran a hand through his thick hair. "Okay. Sure." But when she turned to walk away from him toward the stairs, he grabbed her around the waist and pulled her against him for a passion-rekindling, toe-curling kiss. When he finally came up for air, he gave her a satisfied-looking grin. "I'll see you in the morning." Then he released her and headed off toward the back of the house, his swagger unmistakable.

So he really didn't regret what had happened between them. She wanted to keep it that way. But how? How could she keep him from seeing her as a bad habit he needed to break?

She turned and started up the huge, curving staircase, its polished wood gleaming even in the moonlight and the faint scent of roses from the bouquet in the foyer sweetening the air. With each step she asked herself how. How? Then Dorothy Rivers's words echoed in her head as an answer. *While change can at times be frightening, it is the only way to discover new possibilities.*

Change.

She needed to change. While what she had been through since Harrison rode into her life was staggering, it still wasn't enough. She would take the scholarship and start college. Maybe get a teaching degree. But she not only had to change what she did with her life and where she did it. She also had to change how others perceived her while she was doing it.

Determination and a sense of purpose surged through her as she slipped silently down the hall and into her room. She knew just the person to ask for help.

ASHLEY ONLY BLINKED once over the rim of her morning coffee cup before an unmistakably delighted grin lit her beautiful face in response to Juliet's out-of-left-field question. Fearing that Harrison, or worse, George might make an appearance in the large, sun-washed breakfast nook, Juliet hadn't dared take the time to work her way into asking for Ashley's help any less abruptly.

Juliet still held her breath, though, and waited with nerves strung tight for Ashley to set her cup down and give her answer.

Ashley reached across the white marble tabletop and gripped Juliet's hand. "I would love to help you, Juliet." Her touch was warm and strong and surprisingly reassuring. "Though I don't think you really need to change who you are, to fit in, so much as change your look a little."

She gave Juliet's hand a squeeze before releasing her and sitting back. "Just the other day I was saying how something as simple as a new pair of shoes can completely change the way a woman feels about herself. And how a woman feels about herself is the key to how she projects herself. It's that projection which makes us 'fit in' or not."

Painfully aware of how little cash she had in the Dutch shortbread cookie tin hidden beneath her underwear in her dresser upstairs, Juliet twisted her own coffee cup on its saucer—something she'd never dreamed she'd ever use let alone take pleasure in—and cleared her throat. "I can't really afford much in the way of new clothes, but if you could help me pick out a few key piece—''

Ashley held up a manicured finger. ''Stop right there. You will not be paying for anything.''

Juliet opened her mouth to protest, angry with herself for not thinking of the possibility of Ashley wanting to foot the bill. Ashley shushed her with an impatient wave of her hand that sent her bracelets jingling and mingled her elegant perfume with the pungent scent of freshly ground coffee.

''I want to do this for you, Juliet. Not just because of what you have with my brother but because I like you and I think you deserve whatever sort of makeover you'd like. Besides, I will have a ridiculously good time doing it. So you must promise me that not another word will be said about the expense. Promise?''

Juliet couldn't make that promise, certain Ashley had very expensive taste. ''I can't—''

''Please, Juliet.'' Ashley cut her off again. ''Let me do this for you. For Harrison. He thinks he doesn't need anything but control of the company.'' She made a noise reminiscent of Dorothy's *pish*. ''I've seen the way he looks at you. He's deluding himself. But I'm afraid he's not going to see what's really in front of him unless we knock his corporate socks off. So let me give you a new look that'll blow all his excuses out of the water. All right?''

Nearly brought to tears by Ashley's support, Juliet could only nod her agreement.

Ashley clapped her hands together in delight. ''Fabulous. And I know just where to start.'' She reached for her black leather dayplanner.

Juliet hastened to add, ''I don't want to take up

very much of your time. I know you're really busy getting the retirement party ready.''

Ashley waved her concerns off again. ''Darling, we're women. We can multitask. By this time Saturday at Dad's party you'll be ready to dine with kings and make saints forget their callings.''

THOUGH HARRISON had had every intention of leaving work early for home—the notion of his home being Juliet's and Nathan's, too, sending a surge of what could only be described as giddiness through him—one thing after another had cropped up. And then he'd had to wait for Juliet's surprise to be delivered. It was dinnertime when he finally stepped through the door into the foyer, confirmed by the mouthwatering smells tingeing the air.

Perhaps he'd have enough time before dinner to speak with Juliet about what had occurred last night down by the river. He blew out a noisy breath as he made his way toward the kitchen and family living area looking for Juliet and Nathan. *What had occurred.* Now there was a euphemism. Juliet had rocked his world. Again.

But this time he hadn't allowed his emotional response to make him irresponsible. He'd maintained control. As much control as one could maintain while having one's mind blown, that is. He had halfway hoped making love to Juliet again would take the edge off his need for her.

It hadn't. After just a day without so much as a glimpse of her, his body virtually buzzed with sexual energy. Whatever he had for Juliet, he had it bad. And the worst part was that her refusal to risk getting caught in his bed had started him entertaining crazy notions like marrying her so that her being in his bed would be legit.

How nuts was that?

With no sign of her or Nathan on the veranda, either, Harrison was about to head upstairs when his father emerged from the den, still reading the financial section of the daily paper.

George spared him a quick glance. "Evening, son."

"Evening." While he knew it was probably useless to ask his dad but not wanting to waste time searching the house, he said, "You wouldn't by any chance know where Juliet and Nathan are?"

Without looking up, he said, "Where she apparently belongs."

Stunned, Harrison watched his dad disappear into the dining room. Had Juliet left? Had he so completely misjudged her reaction to their lovemaking last night? A panic akin to the feeling he'd experienced when he'd learned of Nathan's fall swept through him. What had he done? He had to go after her. He turned on his heel and started for the front door. He had to...

Donavon called, "Master Nathan, Juliet. Dinner is ready to be served in the dining room."

Harrison whirled and saw Donavon leaning in the library door. It hadn't occurred to him to look in the formal rooms that opened off the foyer.

Juliet's voice answered from within the library. "Oh. Thanks. Be right there in a jiff, Donavon."

Relief loosened Harrison's muscles with an intensity he chose not to examine. He headed for the library, nodding at Donavon as they passed. Stopping in the doorway of the book-lined room, Harrison's heart tripped all over itself at the sight that greeted him.

Juliet was standing in front of the unlit, mahogany-encased fireplace, an elegantly simple peach dress falling gently from her curves, her head bent over a book she was flipping through, and her soft, sun-kissed hair tucked behind the sensuous shell of her ear before slipping down her back. Her loveliness touched him, making him want to touch her.

A noise at her feet brought his attention to where Nathan sat stacking leather-bound books and reciting numbers not quite in sequence.

Harrison chuckled. ''I guess that's the next best thing to counting cans of beans.''

Juliet and Nathan both looked up at him and smiled. Nathan scrambled to his feet, squealed, ''Dada,'' and ran for his father's legs. As Harrison picked up his baby, he was hit with what had to be the two-by-four of contentment. He could handle coming home to this every day.

Nathan wasted no time finding what was now a permanent supply of licorice in Harrison's breast pocket.

''Hey,'' Juliet greeted him. He hoped it was pleasant memories of the night before that made her color high and her voice husky. ''Guess what? When I came in here earlier looking for something to read, your dad was in here and we got to talking.''

Harrison must have visibly stiffened because she waved a dismissive hand.

''No, it was good. Get this, ol' George and I have something in common.'' She hoisted the book in her hand. ''A love of Shakespeare and other English literature. He has this amazing collection. He said I was welcome to read them.'' Her gaze sliding over the books lining the walls floor to ceiling, she mused, ''Man, I could spend days in here.''

With a pleasant start of surprise Harrison realized what his father had meant when he'd said Juliet was where she apparently belonged. George Rivers thought Juliet Jones belonged in the vaunted Rivers library. *Go figure.*

She returned her gaze to his with an almost shy look. ''And it will be a great place to do my schoolwork.''

Harrison raised his brows. ''Schoolwork? As in college?''

She nodded.

Having learned not to make assumptions about his brown-eyed girl, he pressed, ''You're accepting the scholarship?''

She gave him a sweet smile of reassurance that was like a hole-in-one to the heart. Pleased beyond belief, he grinned back at her. Just when he thought she couldn't make him any prouder with her bravery, she surprised him again. God, she was something.

Clicking steps sounded on the tile behind him and he heard his grandmother call as she approached him, ''Harrison, be a dear and go down to the cellar and pick out a wine to pair with the duck, please.'' She caught sight of Juliet and Nathan and her lovely, lined face lit up. ''Take Juliet with you. Your father's wine cellar is certainly a sight to see. I'll take our angel to the dining room.''

''Certainly, Grandmother.'' He gave Nathan over to her, then held out a hand to Juliet.

Still acting shy, or perhaps self-conscious, Juliet avoided his gaze as she set the book next to the framed photos of the family on the piano before coming forward to take his hand.

He guided her back toward the kitchen and the narrow door that led down into the large, cool wine cellar. His father was quite the collector, and the temperature- and humidity-controlled cellar invariably made it into most tours of the house.

"Did your grandmother say we were having duck?" she asked as she went down the steps in front of him.

He nearly laughed at the trepidation in her voice. "Yes."

"As in *Donald?*"

That did make him laugh. "Trust me, you'll like the way Marie prepares it."

"Mmm," she murmured uncommittingly.

Thinking of all the other times he'd told her to trust him, Harrison changed the subject by explaining how the racks upon racks of wine bottles were organized by type and age, and how wine is paired with food based on the grape's leather and oak tones.

She gave him a look. "So you're telling me that you guys buy this stuff—for a lot of money, I'm guessing—because it tastes like cowhide and wood?"

Chuckling, he corrected, "More like expensive car upholstery and wine barrels."

She threw her head back and laughed, the sound dancing musically amongst the bottles and settling firmly in his chest. It was a feeling he didn't want to lose.

Her eyes twinkling, she nodded solemnly. "Oh. That makes a difference."

His gaze dropped to her lush mouth. Memories of their lovemaking the night before slammed into him.

Sensually wondering if she preferred a sweet or heady taste on her tongue, he asked, "So what would you base your choice of wine on?"

She looked around them at the floor-to-ceiling wooden racks housing hundreds of bottles, then at the larger bottles, still in their lidless crates and lying on their sides on the floor. "Well, I'd decide which one was most in my way, and that's the one that would get killed."

"Okaaay." He drew the word out on a laugh.

"You'd never be disappointed because you'd made the wrong choice."

Thinking how far from disappointed he'd been with her, he took a step closer, reached out and tucked her hair behind her ear. His pulse started pounding. "And if you made the right choice, you'd be pleasantly surprised."

She moistened her lips and he nearly came out of his skin with wanting. "If you were lucky."

"Oh, I think I'm pretty lucky." Suddenly remembering the surprise he had for her, he reached into his pocket. "I have a present for you."

Her brows went up, and when he dangled the keys to the Mercedes SUV in the small space between them, her eyes went wide. "Car keys?"

"And the car that goes with them. Now, before you say anything, I couldn't have you being a prisoner here at the estate. You know you need a way to get around, especially now that you'll be going to school. And if you don't like the color, or heck, even the car itself, we can easily trade it for something else."

Her gaze fastening on the Mercedes logo on the key fob, her expression fell. "My insurance would never cover a car like that."

"It doesn't have to. I'll take care of it." Expecting her argument, he placed a finger on her warm, supple lips the second she opened them. "Because I want to. It makes me happy."

She stared at him a moment more, as if she were searching for answers in his eyes. "Why are you so good to me?" she whispered beneath his finger, sending sparks of awareness clear through him.

He traced her lower lip. "Good? Actually, good isn't the word that springs to mind." *Lustful, insatiable,* yes, but not good.

"Whatever." She took the keys and his hand into hers with a tender smile. "Do me a favor and don't stop just yet."

Extremely happy that she was accepting his gift and liking the way it felt, he lowered his head toward hers, intent on following the same path his finger had taken over her lips. "Don't worry. I don't intend to."

She sighed and her eyes slid closed.

Right before his lips made contact, Donavon's voice echoed down the stairwell. "Do you need assistance choosing a bottle? Dinner is growing cold."

Juliet jerked away with a flustered look. She grabbed the nearest bottle of red wine and held it in front of his face. "Will this do?"

"It'll do," he said, and gestured for her to precede him out of the cellar. Too bad dinner was the only thing growing cold.

HARRISON WAITED until most of the guests had arrived at the retirement party before making his way out onto the veranda, dodging the huge floral arrangements Ashley had insisted upon. He didn't want to appear overly eager for his father to step aside and leave him in charge as the new CEO and chairman of the board. Though everyone knew he'd worked his entire life in preparation for just this moment. Try as he might, he couldn't calm the excited butterflies in his stomach.

Today was the day. Today his father would formally announce his retirement and name Harrison as his replacement as head of Two Rivers Industries. Everything in his life would then be just how he wanted.

Well, almost everything. Ever since their near kiss in the wine cellar, he and Juliet hadn't managed a moment alone together all week. Ashley had apparently recruited Juliet to help with the party planning when she wasn't busy with school-related matters. If only he could lure her back down to the cellar, or to the river bank...

He took a sip of the champagne and stayed back from the closest group of guests, all of whom he knew from work, while he fought to redistribute the blood that had flooded his crotch in response to his thoughts.

He'd also been plagued by the notion that reviving his physical relationship with Juliet was the ultimate irresponsible act. He'd have to be an idiot not to realize she cared for him. Perhaps even deeply. Hell, she was thanking him for being good to her when she should be slapping him for his greed. He just couldn't get enough of her.

And while he wasn't willing to consider what his unrelenting, sometimes aching need for her translated into emotionally, there was no question their relationship couldn't progress to anything formal. The last thing she'd want to try being was a chairman's wife.

Besides, he didn't need any woman in that way, he reminded himself. He had his sister to handle all social arrangements that went with the job, and he certainly didn't need the emotional support many men required to succeed in their careers. He didn't need anyone to bounce difficult decisions off before he made them.

And he never wanted to face the kind of emotional and career evisceration his father had suffered through before and after his mother's death. Harrison never wanted to depend on someone so much that he couldn't function personally or professionally at the same level without her.

Granted, he should probably check for cracks in his own glass house before he threw stones at his dad's, but it had been some time since he'd felt swamped by residual pain from his mother's death. He still missed her—always would—but his life didn't feel quite as empty anymore. Discovering Nathan had apparently healed him somewhat.

How not formalizing their relationship would affect Juliet remained to be seen, though her pragmatism regarding their situation gave him hope that all would be well. Then his life would be damn near perfect.

He had his son, whom he'd been able to entice away from Grandmother enough to play with every day after work. He had Juliet close at hand, though what she had been up to this week he didn't know. And today he would have control of his family's company. He was going to fulfill his mom's dreams for him in the best way possible. As soon as he was made chairman he would complete the purchase of the Dover Creek Mill and increase the assets and revenue potential of Two Rivers by millions.

Close to bursting with satisfaction, he downed the rest of the champagne and headed for the nearest

group of guests. Just as he stepped into the circle of
some upper management people and their spouses a
commotion behind him drew everyone's attention. He
turned and saw something that froze the breath in his
chest.

Ashley had emerged onto the veranda with Nathan
holding one hand and the most stunning creature at
her other side. With noticeably shorter, honey-blond
hair swept sleekly away from her face and flipped up
at the ends, full lips accented by a kiss of muted-red
lipstick, and luscious curves highlighted by a fitted
red suit with big brass buttons, Juliet Jones looked as
if she'd just stepped from the pages of a fashion mag-
azine.

Or through the doors of Saks.

He yanked his eyes from Juliet and narrowed his
gaze on his sister. He'd told Ashley not to meddle,
but clearly she hadn't been able to resist the challenge
Juliet represented. The fact that Juliet had allowed
Ashley to play dress-up with her rocked him back on
his heels. He returned his gaze to Juliet and watched
her scan the crowd. She had really taken his speech
about change to heart.

But why now?

Her searching gaze found him and he saw the answer right there in her eyes. She'd done it for him.
She had allowed Ashley to dress her up and turn her
out like a featured star on *Lifestyles of the Rich and
Famous* to please him.

She had allowed herself to be changed into what
she thought she needed to be to function in his world.

Good Lord, he never would have dreamed that
she'd be willing to try such a stunning transformation.
Though he shouldn't be surprised. He'd seen more

than a few examples of Juliet's courage and determination. Only usually it involved the one person in her world she loved more than her own life—their son.

Their gazes still locked, Juliet gave him a tentative, almost shy smile and Harrison sucked in a breath as realization hit him between the eyes. She'd faced her fear of change for him because of one reason and one reason only. She cared for him deeply, all right. Deep enough to call it love.

Juliet was in love with him, and he didn't know what the hell to do about it.

Chapter Thirteen

Juliet saw the panic flare in Harrison's eyes and suddenly wished she was a stone sinking to the bottom of the river. What had she been thinking to allow Ashley to *unveil* her at George Rivers's retirement party?

Now she had to face Harrison's rejection in front of at least a hundred guests. A hundred people who would look at her and wonder who she thought she was fooling. She had to physically fight the urge to check to see if there was still dirt under her freshly manicured fingernails.

As if sensing she was on the verge of bolting, Ashley sent Nathan toward the waiting arms of his great-grandmother, then touched Juliet's sleeve. She spoke softly so only Juliet could hear. "I think you've suitably wowed them with your looks. Goodness, Harrison appears to have forgotten how to breathe. Now, let's mingle and show them you've got the brains to match the beauty."

Beginning to feel ill over Harrison's reaction to her foolishness, Juliet shook her head. "I can't. This was a mistake."

"No, it wasn't," Ashley insisted, the steel in her

voice belying her serene expression. "This is the perfect opportunity to show everyone what you're capable of, that there's more to you than what they might think."

Juliet swallowed hard against the churning of her stomach, knowing full well Ashley was talking about Harrison. This was Juliet's chance to prove to him in no uncertain terms that she could function in his world, that she wouldn't prove to be an embarrassment. And thanks to his sister's unflagging support and encouragement while she taught Juliet which fork was which and how to interpret the stock page, she knew in her gut she could do it.

The million-dollar question was did he want her to? She chanced another glance his way. Judging from his strangled expression, the answer seemed to be no.

Ashley snagged two glasses of champagne from a passing waiter and handed one to Juliet. "Besides, you already know quite a few of the ladies here from Grandmother's luncheon. We'll start with them. And who knows, maybe you'll drum up more donations for the scholarship fund."

Juliet mumbled, "Donations for the fund. Yes. That's reason enough to stay."

Ashley's smile was brilliant. "Darn tootin' it is. Fund-raising is an art, my dear. Not to mention a decent living, if you can get hired by the right charities." She tugged on Juliet's sleeve to start her into the crowd gathered on the veranda and spilling over onto the expanse of lawn below where the banquet tables were set up. Bumping shoulders with Juliet, she winked and said, "We just might get your future settled yet."

"But I would still like to go to college. You know, on the scholarship."

Ashley's smile grew wider and radiated approval. "You can do that, too."

Overwhelmed by the possibilities being presented to her, Juliet thrust Harrison's displeasure from her mind and gratefully followed Ashley to a group with a few familiar-looking faces.

Mrs. Jacobson spotted them first. She smiled a welcome at Ashley then turned her gaze to Juliet. Her drawn-on eyebrows rose to her graying blond hair. "Oh, my goodness, Ashley. Do tell me my eyes are not deceiving me. Is this Harrison's Juliet?"

Ashley beamed in satisfaction while Juliet inwardly winced at the possessive attached to Harrison's name. But that was precisely why she had no choice but to try and change the way these people perceived her. Whether he wanted her or not, they all considered her *his* Juliet.

Juliet forced a smile and nodded. "Yes, it's me, Mrs. Jacobson."

The older woman shook her head in apparent amazement, and Juliet couldn't help pulling her chin back a little. Sheesh, had she looked *that* bad before?

Mrs. Jacobson said, "My dear, when I first met you, I thought, 'my, what a lovely girl.' Now, all I can think is, 'what a beautiful young woman.' You have blossomed in a mere week's time."

Juliet was about to deny any sort of blossoming and give credit where credit was due, but Ashley stopped her with a discreet bump of her elbow. Her look said, *Just enjoy it.*

Mrs. Jacobson added, "I must introduce you to my husband. He's on the board, you know." With a remarkably deft move, Mrs. Jacobson shifted her plate of hors d'oeuvres to the hand holding her champagne glass and tapped the short, balding gentleman next to her on the shoulder.

He broke off his conversation with another man and looked questioningly at Mrs. Jacobson.

"Alexander, you must meet the young lady I was telling you about." She sent his attention toward Juliet with a gesture. "This is Harrison's Juliet. Isn't she lovely?"

He gave a crisp nod of agreement and, after making the same juggling move his wife had with his plate and glass, he extended a hand to her. "It's a pleasure, Juliet."

Juliet returned his pleasantry while making a mental note to have Ashley show her how to hold a glass and a plateful of shrimp, crackers globbed with decorated pink stuff and tiny little pie appetizers in one hand without dumping it all down her front.

While keeping hold of her hand in his large, rather warm one, Mr. Jacobson said to the slightly younger man he'd been talking to, "Say, she's close to the boy. We should ask her what his plans are."

Ashley looped her arm through Juliet's and pulled her backward just enough to subtly remove Juliet's hand from Mr. Jacobson's clasp. "Sorry, gentleman, but I need Juliet to help me corral Father long enough to present him with his retirement gift."

Mrs. Jacobson gave a dismissive wave of her hand. "George is camped out by the bar. I guarantee you'll have no trouble finding him when you need him." To her husband she said, "Now, what did you want to ask Juliet about?"

Mr. Jacobson gestured to the other man again.

"There are members of the board who are concerned about Harrison's plans regarding this mill he is so set on buying. Would you happen to know if he does indeed intend to entirely shut it down once the sale is complete?"

Ashley shifted forward in a conspiratorial way and said, "Come now, Alexander. Do you really think Harrison has work on his mind when he's with a woman as gorgeous as Juliet?"

Juliet's face flamed.

The other man guffawed. "Ashley, child, your big brother *always* has work on his mind. Never known him not to."

Ashley gave the perfect laugh. "Oh, Walter. That was before he met our Juliet." Then she started to pull Juliet away.

Though embarrassed—and a little flattered—by Ashley's comments, Juliet resisted. Harrison planned to shut down a mill? The ghost of the question she had once asked herself flitted through her mind.

Was the man who held her and Nathan in his arms and made them feel so safe the real Harrison Rivers? Or was he the man who shut down mills, put the almighty bottom line above all else and believed it was never good to love someone too much?

It was past time for Juliet to find out.

"What mill is this?" she asked Mr. Jacobson, surprising Ashley enough that she let go of Juliet's arm.

He met her gaze, his sharp blue eyes clearly assessing her. "The Dover Creek Mill. Not big, but it feeds roughly a hundred and fifty families."

A hundred and fifty families including Juliet's. Willie was to have started working there this week.

She pulled in a steadying breath, but her stomach still knotted. "And Harrison plans to close it?"

Walter joined in. "Not permanently, but it will take a good three years to refit the place the way he wants."

The knot loosened a bit. "He probably intends to hire the mill workers to help with the refitting."

Both men chuckled, but Mr. Jacobson said kindly, "They're mill workers, my dear. Not contractors. Neither union would allow it."

Walter shook his head. "The fact of the matter is the boy likes to make changes, take risks. Always has." He looked at Juliet, then glanced away, but not before she saw what he'd been thinking.

Harrison had taken a huge risk with her, and had paid the price. But when he closed that mill, the families who it supported would pay the price. He had to know that. Or did he? Juliet needed to find out. Willie's future depended on it.

She excused herself from the group and turned to scan the crowd for Harrison. Taller and broader than most around him and wearing a silky brown shirt and tan pants that drew attention to his build, he wasn't hard to spot across the veranda.

At her side Ashley asked, "Juliet?"

"I need to speak with Harrison."

"He knows what he's doing, Juliet."

She looked over her shoulder at the woman who'd surprised the heck out of her by becoming the sister she'd never had and said, "That's what I'm afraid of."

HARRISON WATCHED Juliet make her way toward him with slow and subtle grace. He couldn't help staring.

She was beautiful. And while she had clearly dressed to impress, she seemed completely unaware of the appreciative interest she generated. As a matter of fact, she seemed very determined. Perhaps even angry.

At him.

She wasn't looking at him like a woman in love anymore as she wound her way through the crowd, but more like a woman with a bone to pick.

God help him if she decided to make a scene in the middle of his father's retirement party. Dad definitely would not get over any sort of disruption. While he wasn't sure that his father had even noticed her presence amongst the guests, he certainly would if she did anything unusual.

But the closer she got to him the more she started to smile and nod at the people she passed, particularly the women she'd undoubtedly met at Grandmother's fund-raiser. She looked far too refined to be contemplating a fit, radiating confidence with every step. Damn if she didn't look utterly at home among their guests.

Like she belonged.

While allowing Juliet's emotions to become so deeply involved in their relationship was now his ultimate act of irresponsibility, he didn't regret bringing her here one bit. This was the world Juliet deserved, and he was ridiculously glad to be able to give it to her.

He couldn't help grinning as she came to stand before him. But when he looked into her eyes and saw the hardness there, his grin faded.

She pursed her lips together for a moment, then lifted her chin. "I need to talk to you. Alone."

Fearing that perhaps someone had insulted her in some way, he gripped her waist with a possessive hand. ''What happened?''

''I just…'' She looked away for a second, then straightened her shoulders and looked him in the eye again. ''I'd like to talk to you in private about something. And it can't wait.''

The hair on the back of his neck started to rise with premonition. He feared his perfect world was about to hit a glitch. ''Okay. Let's go in the house.''

Unwilling to let go of her because of a sudden fear she would bolt, he slid his hand to the other side of her waist and guided her toward the French doors. Once in the house he directed her toward his father's study because it was the only room with doors he could close—and lock—on the first floor.

After the doors were secured, he slowly turned to face her, not willing to acknowledge the dread tightening his stomach muscles. ''What's wrong?''

She crossed her arms over her chest, pulling the red fabric of the closely tailored suit tight over her shoulders. ''Are you going to close the Dover Creek Mill?''

Harrison blinked. ''What?''

She shifted her weight in obvious aggravation, and Harrison was momentarily distracted from his confusion by the even more unexpected sight of the shoes she was wearing. They were very red, very high and undoubtedly very uncomfortable. And they struck him as being very, very wrong.

She regained his attention by saying slowly and succinctly, ''Are you, or are you not, planning to close the Dover Creek Mill?''

Confused as hell over why she even wanted to

know, let alone was angry about it, he ran a hand through his hair. "I have to buy it first."

"But then you plan on closing it?"

"So it can be refitted and modernized, yes."

She started to pace, her agitation obvious in her jerky movements and the sharp clicking of her heels on the hardwood floor. "And that will take a few years."

He threw his arms wide and shrugged, "About three, I guess, but what does this have to do with anything? Why do you want to know?"

She abruptly halted and turned to glare at him. "Why do I want to know? Gee, let me think. Maybe it has something to do with the fact that I know—firsthand, mind you—what it's like to be on the other side of a mill closure. I know what it's like to have the powers that be—you, for instance—not give a rat's butt that entire communities are sent into tailspins because the main employer locks the doors—"

"I won't be shutting that mill down for good. And when it reopens, it will be a better, healthier place to work—"

"After three years! What are those people supposed to live on for three years? Anticipation of a better, healthier place to work?"

"Juliet, please. Why are you so angry at me over this?" He looked out the window at the people gathered on the lawn. "Why now?"

"Because I realized that your zest for change affects an awful lot of people, Harrison, and I need to know if you are aware that it's not always for the better."

"I am very aware of my responsibilities. I have always done my damnedest to do the right thing."

"But you interpret doing the right thing to mean growing the bottom line of your company—"

"Which feeds hundreds of people quite nicely, thank you."

"You can do that without putting other people out of work, sparky."

Frustrated by her seemingly unmotivated hostility, he planted his hands on his hips. "Is that so. And you learned how to run a corporation in the course of one conversation? I'm impressed."

"No, right now you're a jerk. A jerk I don't particularly feel like impressing anymore." She bent and yanked the red pumps from her feet.

"You don't have to impress me—"

With an arch look, she interrupted him. "Because I'm bad at it?"

"No, damn it. You've always impressed me, Juliet. From the second I laid eyes on you and saw your ability to find peace in something as simple as the sun on your face and joy in fake flames duct-taped to an old racing motorcycle. And the way you love our son. That impresses the hell out of me. You've even managed to remind me how lucky I am."

He pointed at the shoes she gripped suspiciously like weapons. "You don't have to cram your feet into those things and get all dressed up to impress me. Or anyone. Why don't you go upstairs and change into some jeans and come back down—"

"Oh, I'd come back down, all right, and the smart thing would be to keep going right out the front door. I can't do this after all, Harrison. This," she waved the toe of one shoe at her expensive suit, "is not me. I can pull it off, but I'm not sure I want to. Even at the price of giving all this—'' she indicated the den with both shoes ''—up.''

''But what about Nathan?''

''What about him? You said you love him, but what would you be willing to give up for him?''

One thing he did *not* want to give up was his son's mother. Thinking that it might not be so nuts after all to legitimize his relationship with her, he offered, ''How about if I give up my freedom?''

''What?''

''How about if we get married? You know, so Nathan will be raised in a more traditional family setting.''

''Traditional? Oh, you mean the kind where the dad won't admit to loving the mom because loving someone too much is bad? That kind of family?''

He recognized his own words coming back at him, and, hearing her say them, he realized he didn't like how they sounded. He stared stonily at her. The last thing he wanted to teach his son was that loving was bad. He wanted Nathan to know the joys of love, not the pain. But Harrison's gut twisted with the knowledge that he didn't know how to teach him anymore.

She shook her head and blew out a breath. ''Look, Harrison, I'm sorry. I know you mean well, that this is your way of still trying to fix your mistake the same way you want to fix that mill and make it better. But you're blind to your own needs, just like you're blind to what closing that mill will cost other people.''

''I am not blind to anything, Juliet. I promise you that I'll do everything in my power to make sure no one suffers while I refurbish the mill. And as far as my needs go, why do you think I'm asking you to marry me?''

She arched a brow. "Are we talking emotional needs or physical needs here?"

"Why does it matter?"

Both of her delicate eyebrows jerked high. "You're joking, right?"

He raised his hands in frustration. "What do you want from me?"

"The one thing you won't give me."

"And what, precisely, is that?"

"Your heart."

Said organ froze in his chest. "My heart?"

"Yes, your heart. As in, 'I love you Juliet, with all my heart.' But you won't tell me that, will you? That's not part of your proposal package because you don't feel it."

He clenched his jaw tight. She was asking for the one thing he'd sworn to never give up. Or was she just interested in platitudes? Would she put to words what he had sworn he'd seen in her eyes? Did she really feel it? He turned the tables on her. "So you want a declaration of love. Are you willing to give me yours?"

Her stubborn chin went up. "I think I've given you enough already." She walked up to him and slapped the red pumps into his hands. "I need to make sure that Nathan gets some of your dad's cake before he goes down for his nap. Ashley said ol' George insisted. Go figure." She headed for the door.

A spurt of panic made his heart pound. "Then what will you do?"

She paused at the door but didn't turn around to face him. "I don't know. I've got a lot to think about. But I do know I don't feel like hanging around masquerading as something I'm not." She looked at him over her shoulder and gave him what might have been a smirk if it weren't so heartbreakingly sad. "That whole 'to thine own self be true' thing."

He watched the door shut behind her. He dropped his gaze to the high-heeled shoes in his hands, numbed by the dread oozing through him. What in the hell had just happened here?

The woman you wouldn't admit to loving just walked out on you, sparky.

He shook his head at the irony of her being so entrenched in his life that he heard her in his head, but she wouldn't have him.

He wandered behind the large desk and plopped down in the black leather chair. Setting the red pumps on the green blotter, he studied them as if the answers would jump out of them like cobbler's elves. He was losing it.

"Damn it," he swore in bitter frustration. Why couldn't things have continued the way they were? Why couldn't Juliet be content with what he *could* give her? If she wanted the moon and the stars, by God, he'd arrange delivery. But no, she wanted the one thing he couldn't do.

With an exasperated huff, he propped his elbows on the desk and held his head in his hands, massaging his scalp with his fingers.

Just like his father always did.

A chill claimed him with suffocating swiftness. Here he was, sitting like his dad, feeling useless and bitter. The exact way he had thought he would avoid feeling by making the choice he had thought he should make. The choice of never loving a woman too much.

He'd thought that by holding tight to his heart he'd

be able to escape this fate, that he'd always be in control.

He let loose the loudest snort he was capable of. He hadn't had a shred of control from the moment he'd laid eyes on Juliet. And seeing the hurt in her eyes when he'd denied her his heart left him feeling scraped raw and aching.

He *did* love Juliet and he couldn't imagine living without her. It *was* worth losing control over.

Good Lord, he wanted the family the three of them made more than he wanted anything.

More than he wanted his grandfather's company.

He eyed the shoes on the desk as he rose to his feet. They'd struck him as wrong for a reason. More than anything, he wanted this beautiful, barefoot, brown-eyed girl in his life. He'd be damned if he'd lose her.

AFTER FINDING OUT that Juliet had headed for the river once she'd given Nathan his cake and been assured by Dorothy that she would put the baby down for his nap as soon as he finished eating, Harrison hurried to the boathouse upriver from the dock. What better way to prove to Juliet that he was serious about giving her his heart than from the river she loved?

While he hadn't personally used it in years, the old green canoe had been kept clean and ready to be slipped in the water by the groundskeeper. Harrison had no trouble launching the canoe and hopping in. The current, swift from the summer melt-off of mountain snow, carried him out away from the bank.

Having had no doubts that she would be there, he steered the canoe toward the dock where Juliet sat in the Adirondack, her red suit hard to miss. She was staring at the water, and her forlorn expression tore at his heart. Determination pumped through his veins.

"Juliet!" His shout from the river visibly startled her out of her musing. She jerked forward in the chair at the sight of him paddling toward her.

"Juliet," he called again, and started to paddle backward to keep from passing the dock. The current of the river swirled so that he doubted he'd be able to land the canoe there because of the angle he'd taken.

Rising to her feet, she yelled, "What are you doing?"

He paddled harder. "Losing control, that's what."

"Stop fighting the current. You'll have to cut over to the bank farther down."

"Not of the canoe. Of me! I've lost control of *me*. From the second I laid eyes on you. And I can't fight it anymore. I don't want to."

"What?" She glanced over her shoulder, obviously thinking of the lawnful of corporate stiff-lips over the rise behind her. He followed her gaze, and sure enough, some of them had wandered toward the impressive view the river presented and were now captivated by the spectacle of their boss madly paddling to keep a canoe even with the dock.

Juliet turned back to him and hissed, "Are you nuts?"

"Yes, I'm nuts. I'm nuts over you. I want to be with you, in front of God and everyone!"

Juliet gaped at him, but he couldn't take the time to enjoy her stunned expression. The river was winning the battle, and he drifted past the dock.

"Ah, hell." He gave up and stowed the paddle. Without a moment's hesitation, he dove into the river

toward her. With a few quick strokes he reached the
dock.

She hurried to the edge to help him, but he flattened
his palms on the decking and hoisted himself out the
way he used to do when he had the time and incli-
nation for swimming in the river, then shook himself
like a dog.

"Good Lord, Harrison, what are you doing?"

"Well, proposing to you from the river seemed like
a good idea at the time." He swiped the water from
his face with his hands, then glared at the swirling
water at the end of the low dock. "I forgot about that
damn current, though."

Her glorious brown eyes wide, she quickly glanced
at the steadily growing crowd on the rise and groaned.
"But what will your father say—"

"I don't give a damn." He reached for her and
gripped her upper arms, his wet hands soaking
through her red blazer and sending a shiver through
her. God help him if it was just from the cold. "I
only care what you have to say. So will you?"

"Will I what?"

"Marry me."

"Harrison, we've been through this. You yourself
gave me the courage to refuse to settle for less than
what I want. I'd rather walk away than be with you
knowing you won't let yourself love me." She tried
to pull away from his grasp but he wouldn't let her
go. He couldn't.

"No."

"I won't take Nathan away, if that's what you're
worried about. Is there a carriage house or something
on the estate where Nathan and I can move so he'll
still be—"

"I won't let you walk away from us."

"There is no us," she insisted, and shrugged out of his grasp. She turned away, her determination to resist made dignified by her squared shoulders.

"Yes, there is. There always has been. From the second we first laid eyes on each other, there's been an *us.*" He moved close behind her, the water running off him forming a pool around their feet, making her bare toes curl. He spoke in her ear. "It was there even before. I remember feeling like I was searching for something. At the time I'd thought it was for a way to deal with my grief. But it wasn't. I was searching for the kind of peace that goes beyond being able to accept death. The kind of peace I found with you."

He reached up a hand and touched her shoulder, to solidify their connection. "I felt so centered after being with you."

"I had no idea a visit to the shed had such therapeutic qualities," she scoffed, but she didn't shrug his hand off.

He gave her shoulder a slight squeeze and turned her to face him, angry to hear her belittle what had happened, the way her brother had. "It wasn't that, and you know it. You are the only person on this earth who knows exactly what I mean. We made a connection that day. The kind of connection that can't be broken." He prayed his expression conveyed the depth of his sincerity. If it didn't, he'd have to rage at the moon until she believed him.

"You're a dreamer, Harrison. We could nev—" her voice hitched. "We could never work."

"Damn it, we could. And I'm willing to do anything to make it happen."

"Even trust me with your heart?"

He clasped her delicate hands in his and dropped to one knee. "You already have it, Juliet. I've just been too stubborn to admit it."

She looked out at the river. "Oh, Harrison—"

"I love you. I love you so much I ache." He pulled in a ragged breath. "Say you'll have me."

She closed her eyes and took a deep breath, swaying slightly as the moment dragged on. A tear slipped out and slid down her cheek. He was about to offer her the moon when she whispered, "I'll have you."

Harrison rose and snatched her up in his arms. He crushed her to him, his heart soaring. After a couple of spins, he stopped and nuzzled her soft, honey-brown hair, surprising himself with the strength of his need to hear her say the words. "Do you love me?"

She made an exasperated noise and wrapped her arms tight around his neck. "You jerk. I've always loved you."

He grinned, happier than he'd ever been in his life. "And I you. Ever since I saw you on that balcony, my sweet Juliet."

She pulled back and searched his face, a tentative hope blossoming in her rich, golden-brown eyes. "Why?"

He grinned wider, deciding he was going to find a great deal of satisfaction expressing all his reasons. "Has anyone ever told you that you have *really* sexy feet?"

Epilogue

With the bright, early-autumn sun shining on his slicked-down blond hair, Nathan did a peg-leg skip down the aisle, swinging the satin pillow with its fake gold rings tied on to and fro. He was so adorable in his tiny black tuxedo they could have called it good, after that. But he topped himself by whacking his dad in the legs with the pillow when he reached him at the makeshift altar, then he ran, giggling, to his grandpa George, seated in the first row of white chairs.

From where Juliet stood at the back of the seemingly endless rows of filled chairs arranged on the lawn, she could see her son looking for something inside George's coat. She was just about to snap her fingers at Nat—as if he'd hear her—when he squealed in delight and produced a red licorice stick. Apparently ol' George had decided to start carrying around the key to Nathan's heart. Go figure.

The cadence of the music changed, then the wedding march began. She reached up and checked the French roll her hair had been twisted into for any escapees. It was time. Time for her to walk down the aisle and join her knight, all polished up and shining in his tuxedo armor. He stood tall beneath an arbor smothered in white climbing roses, specially erected for the occasion. The river, with the obliging sun sparkling off its easy-flowing water, made a beautiful backdrop to her dream come true.

Harrison had thought of everything. While Ashley had handled most of the preparations, with Juliet's input, Ashley had sworn that Harrison made a specific request regarding the location of the ceremony. He knew his soon-to-be wife so well. No debutante in the formal rose garden. Nosiree. He was marrying her in view of the river that had brought them together. The river that ran as deep and true as their love.

Tears welled up in her eyes, and Juliet made the trip down the aisle with everything in a blur. Her simple but elegant, off-the-shoulder, white beaded gown swished atop the white satin runner that felt wonderfully cool beneath her bare feet—something else Harrison had insisted on. He'd insisted she ditch the shoes for the ceremony, telling her he wanted to marry her the same way he'd fallen in love with her—barefoot and beautiful. Man, how'd she get so lucky?

She blinked furiously to clear her vision as she approached Harrison, the minister and Willie standing tall and surprisingly well-groomed as best man.

During the three remarkable weeks it took to plan the wedding—and only Ashley Rivers could have pulled it off so quickly—Harrison and Willie had developed an unusual bond. Harrison had asked her brother and a few other mill workers to act as consultants so he could figure out a way to keep the mill operating during refurbishment. She'd never seen Willie so motivated. He'd repaid Harrison with an unflagging loyalty and surprising ingenuity.

A touch to her arm brought Juliet's attention to her mother, seated opposite George on what would have been the bride's side. Dorothy, in her infinite wisdom, had suggested they forgo that tradition so the two sides wouldn't be so glaringly unbalanced in attendees.

Phyllis had cleaned up nicely for the occasion, also, but Juliet still couldn't help hearing the theme song to *Beverly Hillbillies* when she looked at her mom's straw, wide-brimmed hat that didn't quite hide her terminally bad perm. Her far-too-revealing, pink prom-dress-cum-mother-of-the-bride-gown didn't help. But at least she'd come.

Thanks to Dorothy's sudden interest in retail, Juliet's mom had been doing just fine in her newly painted and fully stocked store. The new espresso window with the cute college boys to serve up lattes had been an added bonus.

"You did good, Julie," her mom whispered.

Juliet whispered back, "Thanks, Mom."

While she doubted they would ever be close in the regular mother-daughter sort of way, at least Phyllis was trying. And Juliet was doing her darnedest to meet her halfway. That was a start.

Juliet turned her gaze back to Harrison, and he reached out a hand to her. She shifted her huge bouquet of white roses to one hand so she could slip her fingers, her large diamond solitaire engagement ring winking in the sun, into his warm, gentle grip.

The green-eyed monster of jealousy rearing its head in their toddler, Nathan bailed off from George's lap and shoved his way between his parents. Harrison bent and scooped him up with his free hand, shrugging and smiling when Nat's licorice stick ended up stuck to the front of Harrison's crisp, white shirt.

Juliet met his gaze, and her vision started to swim again from the love shining in his eyes. She had gained so much. All because she took a chance.

And for the second time in her life she got exactly what she'd wanted.

* * * * *

Will beautiful socialite
Ashley Rivers discover true love
where she least expects it?
Find out in
THE RICH GIRL GOES WILD
by Leah Vale,
coming to Harlequin American Romance
in August 2002!

Brides of
the
DESERT ROSE

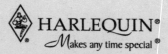

A royal monarch's search for an heir leads
him to three American princesses in

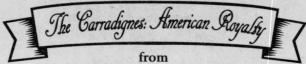

The Carradignes: American Royalty

from

HARLEQUIN®

AMERICAN *Romance*®

King Easton's third choice for the crown is
the beautiful Princess Lucia Carradigne.
Known to all as a New York wild child, this youngest
granddaughter has fallen for the king's royal—and
much older!—adviser. Caught in a compromising
position, will the two marry in name only
in order to avert a shocking scandal?

Don't miss:

THE SIMPLY SCANDALOUS PRINCESS
by Michele Dunaway May 2002

And check out these other titles in the series:

THE IMPROPERLY PREGNANT PRINCESS
by Jacqueline Diamond March 2002

THE UNLAWFULLY WEDDED PRINCESS
by Kara Lennox April 2002

And a tie-in title from

HARLEQUIN®

INTRIGUE®

THE DUKE'S COVERT MISSION
by Julie Miller June 2002

Available at your favorite retail outlet.

HARLEQUIN®

Makes any time special ®

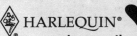

If you enjoyed what you just read,
then we've got an offer you can't resist!

Take 2 bestselling
love stories FREE!
Plus get a FREE surprise gift!